MY
NAME IS
ROSE

a novel

ALEXA KINGAARD

My Name Is Rose
First Edition
Copyright © 2019 Alexa Kingaard
All rights reserved. Printed in the United States of America. For information, address Acorn Publishing, LLC, 3943 Irvine Blvd. Ste. 218, Irvine, CA 92602.

Cover design by Damonza

Book formatted by Debra Kennedy

ISBN – Hardcover 978-1-947392-44-1
ISBN – Paperback 978-1947392-43-4

For my children,
Christopher & Erin.
I love you,
Mom

CHAPTER 1

I recognized all of them. Aging hippies assembled to pay their last respects. Some held toddlers in their arms, their grandchildren who never experienced the communal lifestyle they had afforded their own children. Friends my age, whisked up by parents once intent upon following their dreams of mutual goals and shared ideals. They left the material world in their wake, only to be sucked back into the mainstream lifestyle by the lure of money and shiny new things. I hadn't seen most of them in twenty years.

My husband grabbed my arm as if to steady me, even though I didn't need his assistance. He needed to be needed, and I wanted to be left alone. I didn't feel like being touched, soothed, or consoled – not today.

My two pre-adolescent daughters, named for my mother – her real name – followed close behind and refused to understand the solemn nature of the occasion. What else could I expect? I had severed ties with my parents to pursue what I had convinced myself was an ugly truth, and I waited for their confession to prove me right. It all came too late, and I could blame no one but myself.

"Leave your cell phones at home today," I instructed

Caroline and Nicole before we left the house. I remained in no mood to bargain or argue.

Dual groans of disappointment flooded the air. "I don't want to go to a funeral today. I had other plans. I didn't even know her. Can't I stay home?" Nicole tried her best to squirm out of the obligation, but Andrew extended his hands to both daughters and confiscated the instruments.

"You could have at least warned us. None of my friends will know where I am today. It'll be dark before we get home. Does this mean I can't go to the slumber party tonight?" Caroline's sulky nature emerged, and she didn't hesitate to make her feelings known.

"Don't waste your breath," I overheard Andrew whisper to our eldest daughter. "It won't do you any good."

He projected quiet and calm as usual, but I caught the expression on his face and the stern look he communicated in order to bring Caroline's boil to a low simmer.

We took our seats, beckoned to the front by my Uncle Jacob. Nicole and Caroline were fidgety and restless, and they made it clear they didn't want to be there. Their fingers twitched on invisible cell phones. I could tell they weren't in the moment, and it was all my fault.

"Please settle down, girls," I hushed them. "Try to act your age instead of like petulant toddlers. This is important to me."

As the final mourners streamed in and the room began to quiet, I leaned over and whispered to Andrew, "I have no family. Our children didn't have my parents to call grandparents. I missed out on everything."

He was not sympathetic. "It's too bad you wasted so many precious years chasing this thing. This stupid thing you thought was so important. I love you, Rose, but you have put a thorn smack dab in the middle of your life, of our life. I hope today will bring you some peace."

He was right. I had chased this 'thing' into the ground. Today would be the end of it, or the beginning, depending on how I felt at any given moment. Both anxious and scared, I noticed my father, head down as he tried to stifle his tears. I pictured walking up to him after the service, without the slightest idea of what might happen. I was prepared for anything. I just didn't know what.

CHAPTER 2

"**W**ould you mind checking the garden for some ripe tomatoes, Rose? There will be seven of us tonight, not the usual six."

Glory, my mother, coaxed me to help with Sunday dinner, even though I had tired of the ritual by the time I reached the third grade. It was the same people, every Sunday. I felt bored and impatient with a life – my life – our life – that never seemed to change.

For some reason never explained to me, my mother and father left their parents when they were barely eighteen years old. Both came from good families - pillars of the community, they were called - and attended the best schools in the opulent atmosphere of the City of San Francisco. Their mothers stayed home, cooked, cleaned, cared for the children, did charity work in their spare time, and joined garden clubs.

Their fathers worked long hours to maintain the perception of affluence, often missing out on the best life offered – their families. This had been my parent's childhood, and they both refused to accept the baton being passed to their generation. The idea of community, equitable distribution of workloads, mutual goals, and an idyllic vision of unity and peace captured their imagination and, ultimately, shaped their existence.

I entered the world eight months after the group formed. I always assumed my parents were married. I never asked to see a marriage certificate, and no one ever spoke of a wedding. Everyone but me seemed content to live each day identical to the one they experienced the day before.

I was allowed outside our commune to attend the public schools in the more populated area of town. It energized my spirit and fueled my imagination. It felt invigorating compared to the monotony that beckoned me when I stepped across the threshold of our farmhouse every afternoon.

I dragged myself to the patch of vegetables just outside our back door while Glory watched from the kitchen window. It bothered me that everyone in our community changed their names from what their parents had bestowed upon them to organic, peaceful monikers they felt suited them better - names that would carry them farther in their new pursuit for an unblemished life with shared responsibilities, meals, children, and what I was beginning to suspect, partners. I tried not to think about that, but I couldn't help it when I noticed on Sunday evenings that my father, River, and his best friend, Jacob, sat at either end of the table as though they were both head of the household.

Glory cracked the window and followed my movements as I drifted from one vegetable patch to another. Rows of corn, lettuce, artichokes, carrots, and tomatoes grew in harmony, providing us with a bounty of fresh produce on a daily basis. Fruit trees were prolific, at least an acre that stretched to the bottom of our hill and gifted us in the summer months with a vast selection of peaches, oranges, figs, apples, and pears. I learned to can before I went to school. Of one thing I was sure - I would never go hungry.

"If there are any artichokes left, bring them with you. I still have time to make an artichoke salad before the end of the day." Glory retreated from her watchful perch, returning to her mindless task at the kitchen sink.

"You always have time to make an artichoke salad," I mumbled under my breath. "All the time in the world. What else are you going to do with all those hours in a day?"

I sorted through the vines of tomatoes, beef-steaks and cherry, watching where I walked. The dry, prickly burrs scattered on the ground would bite and dig into the soft soles of my feet if I didn't step carefully. I rarely wore shoes around the commune, and the first thing I did every day when I got home from school was kick them off in the hallway. Sometimes, by Friday, I would have three or four pairs piled on top of each other, but no one seemed to mind. There weren't many rules to live by in our family. Everyone did pretty much what they felt like doing as long as they were considerate of other people's space and feelings. I couldn't argue with the logic.

"Lots of tomatoes. Artichokes have all but disappeared, but I found a few taking their last stand in the garden." I carried the weathered basket, piled high with the vibrant red vegetables, a splash of green peeking through from one robust head of lettuce and the few artichokes that managed to survive. I dropped it on the side counter by the sink. I intended to help, but I still asked my mother, "Would you like me to wash them, Glory?"

We made a strict bargain when I turned eight. She and River didn't want me to call them mother and father, or mom and dad, or mommy and daddy, which sounded strange to my classmates. I had grown used to calling them - all adults for that matter - by their first names. I wished my parents would have allowed me to use their real names. Much nicer, in my opinion. Caroline Nicole and Steven Alexander. A bit old fashioned, perhaps, but it wasn't easy trying to explain to others how my parents became lifetime hippies, content and happy to stay put in one place for their entire lives.

Mother answered, "That would be lovely, dear. I can always use the extra set of hands for Sunday dinner."

I picked the head of lettuce from the basket and peeled back the blemished outer leaves. I set them to one side along with other inedible pieces of vines, roots, stems, and overripe tomatoes. We wasted nothing. We found a use for everything, so I knew better than to throw anything away.

"Who's the seventh? Besides Uncle Jacob, Aunt Fern and Destiny? You said there would be seven tonight. Anyone I know?" I was curious. I considered any injection of novelty a welcome relief from the usual routines.

"Jacob's brother was in a farm accident, almost lost his arm." My mother looked down at the pot filling with water in the sink. She shook her head before she continued. "His son, Andrew, will be staying with Jacob, Fern and Destiny for a few months while his father heals. His mother has her hands full with his younger sisters, going back and forth to the hospital. Doctors say it'll be at least a year before he's back to normal...arm was pretty much severed and crushed when his tractor rolled over him as he tried to dislodge a tree branch."

I felt the blood drain from my face at the thought of the horrific sight. I pulled the stool from beneath the counter. I steadied myself, overwhelmed by a rush of sorrow. "How did that happen? Wouldn't you know better than to keep the engine running?" I prodded. I felt sad for Uncle Jacob's brother and his family, even as I tried to picture something so awful. "Seems like anyone in charge of such a massive piece of machinery would be more careful."

"Don't you go and say anything," Glory cautioned. "I don't know all the details, but I think Andrew shifted into the driver's seat right after his father jumped out of the tractor to move something out of the way. The field was full of debris. He bent down to pick up a log and heave it to one side. Andrew thought he had jumped clear, but his father went back under the tire to dig out one large branch that was jammed tight. Andrew put the tractor in gear." Glory drew a deep breath. "If it wasn't for Andrew, his father would've probably lost his arm. He had the quick wit to apply a tourniquet and stop the bleeding. He kept him alive until the ambulance arrived. He's still pretty shook up, even though it happened four weeks ago. Best for him to get out of there for a while."

"That's horrible! I hope he knows it wasn't his fault." My eyes watered as I imagined what I might do if something like that ever happened to River or Glory, especially if I had been the cause. I finished the salad, rinsing, slicing, and dicing each vegetable with measured care. I wanted to help Glory more than ever at this moment and enjoy this Sunday ritual as much as she did. I didn't know what I would do if anything ever happened to my parents.

"Is there anything else I can do for you before everyone gets here?"

Glory shook her head. She continued to roll out her famous buttermilk biscuits with a wooden rolling pin, then cut into the soft dough with a sharp-edged knife, each biscuit the exact same size as the one before. She placed them, one at a time, on the cookie sheet with deft precision and basted them with the melted rosemary butter that bubbled to perfection on a low flame. She slid them into the oven and within minutes, the whole house filled with the familiar aroma of Sunday dinner. I moved closer to my mother, surprising her with a hug that enveloped her petite frame.

I always envied her diminutive stature, mine being more sturdy and thick. My friends said I looked athletic, whatever that means. Neither of my parents were large people, but they teased there was a tall Norwegian Viking lurking somewhere in our family tree. I seemed to be the likely descendent, since at fourteen years of age, I stood five-feet, six-inches in height. I towered over the rest of the girls in my class, and was still growing.

"Thank you, Rose. I think we've done about everything that needs doing. You've been a big help." Mother smiled as she tidied up the sink, gathered the vegetable peelings and eggshells, and carried them out to the mulch area for future gardens to flourish.

CHAPTER 3

No one ever knocked on our door and strangers were rare. By six o'clock our Sunday dinner guests arrived, each settling into our well-worn recliners and aging sofa.

Andrew entered last. I could tell he was waiting for an introduction. Aunt Fern and Uncle Jacob must have felt he needed none, and his cousin, Destiny, seemed not to know if she should speak up or keep silent. Destiny and I attended the same middle school. Eager to move on to high school next year, we shared the same classroom, friends, and teachers. Andrew looked to be near our age, maybe a little older. He moved past me, joining the men on the couch in silence.

I waved in his direction and managed a weak, "Hi. I'm Rose."

Aunt Fern was the only one to react. "Where are my manners? I'm so accustomed to being around all of you, I forgot to introduce you." She turned to her nephew, and I noticed the pained expression on his face as he tried to get comfortable on the couch between his uncle and my father. "So sorry, Andrew." She pointed in my direction. "That's Rose. She goes to school with Destiny, and they're only one month apart. Glory and I were pregnant at the same time."

Is that necessary information? I wondered.

"And this would be Uncle River and Aunt Glory." Aunt Fern pointed out my mother and father. "None of us are related by blood, but if you're not a parent, you're aunt and uncle. No one planned on giving titles to each other when the commune was created, but that's how it evolved over time." Aunt Fern smiled, brushed aside wild, mahogany-colored curls that had fallen into her face, and joined my mother in the kitchen.

I felt uneasy, uncertain about what to say to this new addition to our Sunday dinners, a weekly ritual since Destiny and I were in pre-school. Even she appeared to be ill at ease. I wondered how she felt about her cousin, her boy cousin, coming to live with her. I hoped it was for a long time. I thought he was cute.

He repositioned himself between the two grown men. He looked anxious. Who wouldn't be? Even though he was used to farm life, communal living was far different and would take some adjusting. My observant nature guided me to scrutinize the scene, Andrew with his long legs stretched out underneath the coffee table, and River sitting up straight, shoulders back, in an effort to stretch out to his full height. This was the first time I felt he may have been bothered by his stature, not short at five-foot-nine, but next to Andrew and Uncle Jacob, the difference was evident.

I decided to start a conversation, no matter how awkward. "How long will you be staying here, Andrew?"

I offered him a glass of water, which he took. He seemed relieved that he had something to hold. It was obvious he wasn't a stranger to farm chores. I noticed callouses on his hands. Then, I remembered. It had to be difficult for him. I pondered what he might be thinking when he responded in a flat monotone, "That would depend on when my dad gets home. He's in the hospital." I didn't let him know that I knew.

We locked eyes. "I'm sorry, Andrew. Well, Destiny and I can keep you company. Will you be going to school with us?"

"How old do you think I am?"

I did my best to sound engaging. "Well, you're pretty tall, and I figured you might be in high school, but I'm tall, too, so you never know." I felt foolish. Of course he looked older than we did, with muscles well-defined from the farm chores, a tell-tale sign of stubble that appeared to need regular shaving, and forearms that were a golden brown from the hours he spent in the sun.

"A junior. I'm a junior in high school. Could be I'll be finishing second semester here."

Destiny chimed in, "Middle school and high school are on the same block. Town's not very big. We can all take the same bus."

Destiny was beautiful. I turned in her direction when she started to speak, thinking how flawless her features appeared compared to mine. Her long, velvet brown hair was the same color as her mother's. Perfect almond-shaped eyes, the deepest chocolate brown hue, reminded me of Hershey's syrup. Her smile could light up a room, and she'd begun to understand how all these attributes could win her the attention of every boy in school. She favored her mother's side of the family, Uncle Jacob being of sturdier stock, and a thick head of dark brown hair that hadn't seen a pair of scissors for at least three years. He had brown eyes. I had brown eyes. River's and Glory's eyes were blue.

I could smell the heavenly aromas coming from the kitchen. The stove, a cast-off from better days in someone else's house and notable for its olive green drab color, was in perfect condition. River and Uncle Jacob knew of a particular junkyard where all the wealthy people discarded their worldly possessions when they tired of the color, shape, or size, most outdated in five years or less. They made regular trips, eventually finding whatever we needed. They didn't think they should ever have to pay for anything, as long as it was discarded. Whether cheap or frugal, I didn't know yet, but it made me feel poor - too many hand-me-downs and nothing ever crossed our doorway with a price tag on it. Even our bathtub was salvaged, along with most of our furniture. Destiny's house was the same. Our trips to Good Will and second-hand stores in town didn't hold the same allure for us as they had when we were younger. When I asked Glory for a new pair of jeans or tennis shoes, she always reminded me that money didn't grow on trees.

Yet for all their self-denial, River and Glory seemed content. Uncle Jacob and Aunt Fern appeared blissfully happy, as well. As I became more and more aware of my surroundings, I felt neither content nor blissfully happy. Most of the time I was bored and wondered if I would ever experience the world that beckoned beyond the commune. As much as my parents wanted to escape the outside world, I longed to join it.

CHAPTER 4

Rain. It rained almost every day between December and April, the sun making an uncommon appearance every now and then. I could almost appreciate River and Glory's choice of putting down roots in the Pacific Northwest, a verdant valley just over the Washington state line. It was an obvious choice in their youth, an idealistic group of recent high school graduates and college drop-outs, who abandoned their worldly treasures in search of a simple, pure existence, carved from the land, ingenuity, and hard work. They all felt they had something to prove to themselves, their families, and the world. Life, they thought, didn't need to be complicated.

With Mother Nature's never-ending supply of water, combined with the right amount of sunshine, they grew and cultivated enough fresh produce, not only for themselves, but for sale at a roadside stand, built, stocked and operated by the members of the commune. Frequented by locals and travelers, their reputation grew for the ripest fruit, tastiest vegetables, and fairest prices. They worked the forty acres they collectively purchased when the group started, which made it possible for them to avoid regular jobs in the world outside their protected lifestyle.

Some of the members had trust accounts started by their wealthy parents on the day of their birth. Although meant to pay for a college education, there wasn't anything mothers and fathers could do once their babies turned eighteen and the investment accounts were rolled into their names. Others worked on their summer breaks during high school and had small savings they earned themselves. Glory, River, Uncle Jacob, and Aunt Fern arrived with the clothes on their backs. They promised to buy in with sweat equity, labor longer hours than the others, and clear the land for future cabins that would house the entire group.

Before my birth, almost one hundred people joined Glory and River in order to make our community a reality, but each year the population steadily dwindled. By the time Destiny and I were toddlers, a total of eighteen adults, thirteen children, four goats, two cows, one horse, twenty chickens, and six pigs co-existed on our land. Families grew weary of the hard living conditions they once perceived as idyllic, and most connected sufficiently with the outside world to recognize the advance of technology in mainstream society. One by one, they packed their belongings to return to their parents' homes, a broader and brighter education for their children, and a more hospitable landscape. When Destiny and I started school, two more families had left, further diminishing the headcount of friends, neighbors, and playmates.

I remember the conversation about whether Destiny and I would join other children, or be forced to endure the homeschooling whims of our parents. We hadn't attended kindergarten, although our parents made sure we knew how to read. That was the extent of our scholarly instruction.

"What do you think about starting the girls in public school?" Aunt Fern asked at our Sunday dinner table.

For those who had remained behind, it was up to each individual parent to make this decision. All, so far, had opted to educate their children on their own, with little supervision and no apparent curriculum to ensure a proper head start to their studies.

"School starts next month. Should make a decision pretty soon." As Aunt Fern passed the potatoes to Uncle Jacob, Destiny and I swapped glances. Even at six years old, we knew enough to do our best to protest our fate.

"I want to go to school," Destiny piped up.

I followed with what sounded like more of a whine. I didn't want to miss out on all the playground equipment we spied on our infrequent trips to town, and I longed to participate in a life beyond our seclusion. I looked first to Glory, then to River. "Please, please, please??? Can we go to school? There's nothing to do around here!" I excelled at whining, or so I had been told.

River patted my head and smiled. "Okay, Rose, we'll think about it." He cast a questioning look at Glory, who in turn passed the remaining dinner platters to her left like she always did. Each one took a helping before we nodded our heads in thanks.

Aunt Fern buttered her biscuit with a precise wave of her knife and spoke with conviction, "Oh, Glory, I don't see anything wrong with sending the girls to school in town. It'll be good for them to meet other children." Aunt Fern flashed Destiny and me a big grin, and we couldn't help but return it with smiles of our own. I remember like it was yesterday. My first glimpse of freedom.

Uncle Jacob and River nodded their agreement, concerned more with the ham passing under their noses than whether or not we would be educated by the public school system or by our mothers. Glory shrugged, outnumbered, and squeezed my hand. I jumped from my seat and planted a big kiss on her cheek, the one way I could let her know how much being a part of the outside world meant to me.

UNLIKE MOST KIDS OUR AGE, Destiny and I couldn't wait for summer to end. The anticipation of going to school was all we talked about once our parents decided they would give it a try. We spent countless hours in our apple grove under one particular tree, which shaded us on the warmest of days and provided a view of the creek that ran through the property. With the constant rain during the winter, it never dried up and the sun's beams created sparkles that danced on the surface and shone like precious jewels.

Every day, Glory and Aunt Fern made us lunches of peanut butter and jelly sandwiches, fresh carrots from the garden, and a large cluster of purple grapes. Packed in brown paper bags, they wrote our names with a red crayon - like it made a difference. The lunches were identical, but we delighted in the fact we looked like school girls. Sometimes we drank the icy water from the creek, and never minded we didn't have a cup. We scooped up the shimmering, iridescent liquid with our hands, and on the hottest of days, we splashed in the ankle-deep water to cool off.

We played on our own, every day spent in the same spot. And even though it was a good mile in each direction, we were familiar with the path. Looking back, I admire my parents for trusting us and everyone else who lived in our commune, trusted we would be home by dark, which we were every day, and trusted no harm would ever come to us, which it didn't.

CHAPTER 5

I barely had enough time to finish my breakfast and gather my books before I bolted out the door. For some reason, on this morning, I felt an urgent need to spend time choosing my outfit rather than packing a lunch.

Dinner with Andrew the night before created a sense of urgency to look the best I could possibly look before we met at the bus stop. I had already planned what I would wear. *Something different, something not so heavy.* It was almost spring, and I hoped for a little bit of sunshine and an excuse to wear a lightweight sweater that showed my curves. Like the emergence of a new season, my body had started to develop under a layer of thick flannel, corduroy, and the bulky farmer's jacket meant for nothing else than to keep me warm.

I'm sure he didn't think of me at the dinner table. Most of the talk centered on his father's accident, a matter of fact conversation for the adults. I watched Andrew squirm in his chair. He endured the conversation but never engaged.

I managed to alleviate the situation by interjecting something about school and meeting at the bottom of the hill in the morning. I think he was grateful. I was smitten and felt an unfamiliar stir in the pit of my stomach as I watched him pick at his food, his mind a thousand miles away with his father and family.

I looked across the table at Andrew. "Meet you guys at the bus stop tomorrow?" I asked.

"Me? I'm sorry, I didn't know you were asking me. Yeah, sure." Andrew looked distracted. His food remained untouched, save for the crumbs of three of my mother's biscuits, a testament to their power to comfort even in the most stressful situations. He turned to his cousin for additional information. "What time?"

Destiny, relieved for the change of subject, perked up at the thought of the three of us boarding the bus together. If nothing else, it would give us something else to talk about after school when we did our homework together.

"We'll meet you at seven, regular time." She turned in Andrew's direction, putting down her mashed potatoes-filled fork. "The bus drops you first. Middle school is a few more blocks further down the road. We'll see you on the bus in the afternoon, after school."

I could tell Andrew was not enthusiastic about taking a public school bus with two adolescent girls still in middle school, but he was polite. I thought I saw a shy smile emerge as he responded, "Sure, girls. Guess that's the schedule for the next few months."

He turned to me without expression, "I'll know my way around better after tomorrow. Then you two won't have to stick so close."

"Oh, I don't mind!" I sounded too eager, immediately recoiled, and re-focused on my dinner plate. I wasn't hungry and my stomach continued to churn.

IT WAS DIFFERENT TAKING the bus with Andrew. Destiny slid into the last open seat, ample for two, cozy and crowded for three, especially given that her cousin was almost six feet tall and had to position himself on the edge of the tattered and worn leather seat. I sat squished between the two of them. When Andrew's leg couldn't avoid brushing against mine, my stomach flipped in an unfamiliar way.

I could barely breathe, but managed, "I hope you'll like your new school, Andrew. Destiny and I can't wait to get out of middle school. I already feel too old for all those children running around on the playground." Two weeks ago I was one of those children, but now, sitting a hair's breadth from Andrew, I knew that was all in my past.

"It'll do. I don't have a choice, do I?"

He looked resigned. I knew he couldn't tell what I was thinking. He just stared past the trees, past the stop signs, past the signals on the main highway as we all approached our destinations. I didn't want to see Andrew disembark first, knowing Destiny and I would be taking the bus to the end of the line.

Walking towards the school entrance, I felt I had already surpassed the immature boys that dodged and darted around us in an effort to get our attention. They made silly faces, jabbed at one another, and told crass jokes loud enough for us to overhear. Destiny and I both cringed.

In a momentary lapse of good judgment, I mumbled, "Your cousin is so cute."

We hurried past the other students and made our way through the massive double doors. "How did I miss that?"

Destiny thought joking with me would somehow make me want to continue the dialog, but instead, I felt the opposite and changed the subject.

"I hope he'll be okay today, that's all I meant. New school and everything."

"Why wouldn't he be? He's a big boy. Do you have a crush on him or something?" Destiny wouldn't let it go and talked right until the last bell that signaled the beginning of the school week and an end to our conversation.

I was thankful. I wasn't sure I was ready to share my thoughts or feelings, not even with Destiny.

"You look flushed, Rose. How was your day?"

I couldn't admit to anyone, especially not to Glory, that I had dawdled away the last eight hours daydreaming and thinking about Andrew. I deflected Destiny's questions and prodding throughout the day. She finally dropped the subject, but in my mind, it was all settled. I would one day be Mrs. Andrew Fletcher.

CHAPTER 6

By the time spring was in full bloom, so was my heart, but I managed to keep my deepest thoughts to myself. I sorted and sifted through my functional wardrobe. I threw out every oversized, plaid, flannel shirt, along with an assortment of ill-fitting jeans, mostly men's. They served no useful purpose other than keeping me warm during the cold, wet winters. They were incredibly unattractive.

I begged Glory to take me to Good Will one Saturday afternoon. To my surprise, she obliged. She asked River to make sure there was plenty of gas in the old truck, rusted from years of exposure to snow, rain, and sun, the once fire-engine red color reduced to an orangey, peeling shell. The tires were almost bald. River and Uncle Jacob had been on the lookout for over a year, hoping as if by magic to discover a set of four brand new tires that would fit their truck – tires abandoned in the junkyard and waiting to be hauled away.

I said something about their thriftiness one evening at dinner. "Why don't you just take some money from the fruit stand profits and buy a new set of tires?"

I was incredulous that they would risk their lives, or the lives of others, for the purpose of getting something for free instead of paying a fair price for a very important purchase. River looked more surprised than upset, and the corners of his mouth turned up into a smile. He let me finish.

"I'm almost old enough to drive. Those tires aren't very safe."

I stated my case without emotion, hand-wringing or arm waving. I tried to remain respectful, but my parents had become so accustomed to scrimping by with nothing more than the bare necessities, I wasn't sure if it would spark a memory in either of them. A memory of their first time getting behind the wheel. They didn't talk much about their youth, but I did have enough information to know they'd been raised in traditional households, attended upper-class high schools, and behaved as every other teenager has while grappling with the inevitable emergence of adulthood.

"Glory, how old were you when you got your license? I bet not much older than me." I caught a glimpse of her expression at that moment, and I witnessed one little flash of reminiscence as I watched my mother tilt her head as if to summon a memory from her past.

"You're right, Rose. I wasn't much older than you." She stopped, savored the recollection with a slight expression of melancholy, and jolted herself back to the present. "I learned to drive in the streets of San Francisco. Your grandfather, my father, bought me what was supposed to be the newest innovation in affordable automobiles, perfect for a first car, especially a girl. It was a Ford Pinto, light blue, two-door, fastback sedan. They advertised it as the 'Little Carefree Car.' I didn't care what they called it, I loved that car. I drove it for two years. It was my birthday present...my sixteenth birthday."

"What happened to it?" I had never seen it, assumed it

had been left behind, but I still hoped for a response.

Glory sighed, sounding resigned. I thought I detected an ounce of remorse in her tone. "Didn't need it. Left it parked in front of my parent's house when River, Jacob, and Fern and I set out for our new home." She pursed her lips, shook her head in slow motion, and changed the subject.

I wondered if that was the whole story. I doubted that it was.

I pushed back my chair and toyed with a fresh slice of bread she had baked that afternoon. Glory could cook, Glory could bake, and Glory could can. Glory could grow the most magnificent fruits and flowers from seed. I picked apart the soft dough, listening as my mother recalled that eventful moment in her life. It sounded like a wonderful life. What made it so bad that they left it all behind?

River just listened, devoured three slices of bread, topped with butter and fresh peach jam, and allowed the conversation to go where it might. If he felt uneasy, he didn't let on.

I relished the rare telling of my mother's childhood. Sometimes it seemed as though neither of them had ever been young.

"You might not recall, you were so little, but River and I took you to the City to visit my parents one Christmas. It was a long time ago."

Yes, she definitely changed the subject.

"Was that the big house on the hill squeezed in between all the other houses? They looked like they reached the sky and I felt dizzy, like I was going to fall down. I couldn't believe how many stairs there were, first to the front door, then up one flight, and then another to get to the living room. The whole house smelled like gingerbread."

"It always smelled like gingerbread during the holidays. My mother loved to cook. Seems like my father was never home. He worked a lot."

Glory's voice grew softer and smaller as she continued.

I interrupted. "I remember having hot cocoa under the tree and getting cookies ready for Santa." I stopped, the picture in my head so clear even though I'd only been three years old. I heard an audible sigh from Glory and noticed that her bright blue eyes dulled with the recollection. I feared I had started something I shouldn't have.

"You Okay, Glory?" River interjected and managed a protective glance towards my mother. He turned to me. "For Christ's sake, we were talking about tires. How did we get here?"

I knew the question was meant for me, not Glory. I had struck a nerve, but my mother calmed the awkward moment and persisted.

"It's all right, River. We never have talked about this, and Rose is old enough now."

I picked up the discussion again, eager for the story that would evolve. "I remember a little bit of that night. Grandma, you, and River were rushing back and forth, trying not to talk too loud, but I could tell something was wrong. You were crying. You would come back out to the living room to be with me, sit by the fire, help me get ready for Santa and you would smile, then cry. I hadn't thought about that Christmas until now. I'm not even sure it was real."

"It was real." Glory stood, moved towards the couch and settled herself comfortably in the deep corner of the well-worn cushions. River watched us both, never a fan of confrontation or bad news.

"Your grandfather was very ill. He wanted to spend one

last Christmas with us in the house. He died three days later. When all of his paperwork was in order, we were not prepared for what we found."

I could tell this was hard for Glory to talk about. She never looked up.

"While my mother was under the impression there was plenty of money and she wouldn't have to struggle financially, quite the opposite was true. My father had lost everything the previous year, might be why he got so sick. My mother was none the wiser. He spent a lifetime achieving and amassing, providing both of us with the best that money could buy, and with one bad investment in the stock market, everything was wiped out. He never talked to my mother about it, but he hadn't made the house payments in a year. The bank had already started foreclosure proceedings a few months before he died. His life savings were drained, every investment was worthless. If not for a long forgotten life insurance policy, which made it possible for my mother to hold on to the house, she would have been out on the streets."

Glory shook her head as she continued. "It was all for nothing. He worked himself day and night to reap a fortune, living an enviable lifestyle with big cars, a vacation home in the mountains, country club memberships...but he never saw his family. Money drove him, not me, not my mother. I think I missed him as much when he was alive as I did after he died."

My head swam with unanswered questions, but I decided not to push. I would ask again in time. "So what about teaching me to drive, River?" I knew how to change the subject, too, and it was obvious that River was more than ready to move on to another topic.

"I think it's a good idea, Rose. Saturday, before you and

Glory go to town. I'll see what I can do about the tires." He nodded at me as he pushed his chair back from the table, stood, and excused himself from the uncomfortable conversation.

CHAPTER 7

It took a while, but I finally mastered the art of driving a four-on-the-floor stick shift. River said if I could learn to drive the old truck, I would be able to drive anything, even if I was still a year away from getting my learner's permit. He and Uncle Jacob chipped in for a set of retread tires, setting them each back about fifty dollars, but even Aunt Fern and Glory expressed their thanks.

There are times when nothing but money will solve a problem. I never felt more aware of that fact than when my mother and I prepared for the Goodwill outing. Almost everything in my closet screamed tomboy. I wanted nothing more than to replace it all with a more attractive wardrobe, one that would make the opposite sex take a second look when I walked past them in the hall, or set me apart from the group of girls sitting at the lunch table.

Destiny didn't need to change a thing about her appearance, personality, or style. She made it look effortless. If I hadn't loved her like a sister, I would have been jealous.

Andrew grew accustomed to Destiny and I seated beside him on the school bus every morning, and again every afternoon. No amount of hair brushing, a more feminine style, or warm smiles made him notice me any more than he had on his first day of school. He would wave us off the bus in the morning, and he never said much on the ride home in the afternoon. Still, knowing I would see him twice a day, five days a week, and at Sunday dinner added a new dimension to my monotonous life.

During an unseasonably hot week in April, all of the girls shed their bulky sweaters for sundresses and sleeveless blouses. As long as our arms were covered, we were allowed to wear them during school hours. Once the last bell rang, most peeled them off their shoulders and shoved them into their book bags, giggling with girlfriends in small groups. The boys formed a circle in the distance, and they gawked at the emerging womanhood displayed on their campus like a bunch of lovesick puppies. None of them had mastered the art of subtlety, a trait many of them never perfected even as grown men.

I grabbed a seat next to the window so I could get the best view of Andrew as he approached the bus. I watched with silent anticipation as the stride of his long legs brought him closer to the open doors, and then I scooched myself into a compressed position to make the empty space beside me appear open and available.

Destiny figured out my hopeless daydream about Andrew after the first week. She left me to continue my fantasy while she basked in the attention of a different boy every day, each one competing for her presence on the way home from school.

"Andrew, wait up!" A tall, beautiful high school girl, highlighted strands of blonde bangs falling into her eyes, shouted at him as he took the first step into the half-full bus. Breathless from her sprint, color bloomed in her cheeks and added a natural glow to her already flawless complexion.

He waved, smiled at her, and continued his path down the narrow aisle, passing his cousin, and not offering so much as a nod in my direction.

She squeezed past me and Destiny. She made a beeline for Andrew, who grabbed the last seat in the back as he motioned for her to join him. I saw him smile. I had never seen him smile quite like that before. He ignored Destiny and me all the way home. It became clear that only one person had captured his attention.

I tried to block out the sounds of her forced laughter, and the "Really, Andrew? That's so funny! Tell me more!" She sounded loud and obnoxious, as if she wanted to make sure everyone heard their conversation.

My heart sank, and it was all I could do to keep from crying. I didn't say a word as the bus driver maneuvered the back roads, dropping students at their doors and corner bus stops. I buried my head in a textbook to keep my mind from wandering.

The open farmland was wrapped in a lustrous layer of color with the sudden appearance of flowers that bloomed in abundance. The enormous oaks displayed a rich canopy of new life after a long, wet winter. As a little girl, I was fascinated with their 'fruit', as Glory called them. She was never able to convince me that acorns were anything more than squirrel food and certainly not fruit by my standards. I lived in fear that one day I would see a mound of them on my oatmeal instead of berries or peaches, and my mother would insist that they were edible.

What if I cracked a tooth? What if I couldn't chew it and had to swallow it whole? I had prepared myself to turn blue and gasp for my last breath at the breakfast table should I ever be urged to test my theory. I wondered if Glory ever knew of my acorn insecurity, or that she had instilled a terrifying vision in the heart of her little girl. Probably not.

Any other time, this reflection would have made me grin. At the moment, I felt nothing but disdain for the spring bounty as we approached the familiar stop at the bottom of our hill.

The doors of the bus swung wide. I bolted through them without acknowledging Destiny or the driver. Andrew took all three steps in one, long leap, then moved to one side to allow the bus to pass. I turned to look at him long enough to see him wave an enthusiastic good-bye to the blond beauty, her face pressed against the window, both of her hands cupped to her pursed lips, and blowing melodramatic kisses in his direction.

"YOU'VE BEEN QUIET LATELY. Anything bothering you?" Glory showed concern every time she sensed an emotional lull, but she remained clueless as to what I suffered or thought during that time.

Andrew paid little or no attention to me after that day on the bus. I was crushed. I knew I would never mend. I hoped he would go back home before Destiny and I went to high school the next year, but it was looking like he might be staying through the summer. *"Please be gone before I go to high school,"* I prayed every night, uncertain if it would do any good. That was the least I could ask for. I knew it would never be me that Andrew dreamed about. The blonde took up all of his free time, the object of his high school affections.

"I'm fine. No need to worry about me," I lied.

"There's one last Sunday dinner before school's out for the summer, and Andrew asked if he could bring a friend. A nice girl he met a couple months ago. He seems to be doing well and adapting to the new school. Won't that be nice?'

How long would I have to keep up this charade?

I steadied myself as I envisioned our Sunday dinner table encroached upon by an interloper, my rival for Andrew's affections. Unwelcome by any stretch of the imagination. The lump in my throat made it hard to respond in more than barely a whisper, "I don't know why we need to rock the boat with our Sunday dinners. Andrew was enough of an intrusion, now he's bringing a friend? From town?"

I pushed past Glory, taking the stairs two at a time in an effort to make it to my bedroom before I broke down in front of her. She followed, or made an attempt. With a wet dish towel still wrapped around a half-dried frying pan, she tried to coax me out of my bedroom. She also made a valiant effort to soothe whatever ailed me, but I wasn't interested in engaging her or anyone else in conversation. I heard her footsteps retreat as I curled up into a ball and buried my head in my pillow to muffle the tearful sounds of my broken heart.

When I finally did join my mother downstairs, all I noticed was her beautiful, angelic face, perfect without makeup, and naturally sun-streaked blonde hair cascading over her eyes. She covered her body with loose-fitting clothes, but I could tell she remained shapely and firm. Her blue eyes were perfect in shape, open and alert, and the mirror to her soul. I always knew when she was happy, or sad, or upset, which wasn't often.

River's eyes were equally as blue, but lighter, almost translucent. I questioned how I could have been created with these dark chocolate colored eyes from two blue-eyed parents.

I learned about dominant and recessive genes in Biology. Two blue-eyed donors couldn't possibly produce a brown-eyed child, but a brown-eyed parent could have a blue-eyed child.

My teacher insisted that if a child is born to a blue-eyed mother and a blue-eyed father, then one of them is not the biological parent. I kept this information to myself, but knew there would come a time when I would need to ask. Uncle Jacob had brown eyes, a dominant gene. I couldn't help thinking that this peaceful retreat, our commune, may have started out as much more.

I HOPED MY EYES did not appear puffy from crying as I joined my mother, sitting by herself on the couch. I didn't feel like answering questions or being probed for information I didn't want to share. All I did want was to banish Andrew from my thoughts and stay as far away from him as possible. I pushed my school books and binder to one side, along with a stack of clothes that should have already been put away, and tried to make room for the two of us.

"I think I might be getting the flu," I lied.

Glory gave me a hug, felt my forehead with the palm of her hand, and agreed, "You do feel a little warm. Why don't you stay downstairs and rest while I finish dinner? We can talk about Sunday another time."

I watched her, in all her dainty perfection, return to her chores in the kitchen that was soon filled with aromas of roasted chicken and fresh peach pie. I let my mind wander and pondered if I would ever know my real father's identity, or if I would ever possess the courage to ask.

CHAPTER 8

"What are you going to do after high school?"
Destiny and I decided to spend our last weekend before graduation at the stream where we had spent endless hours as children, dreaming about our futures, talking about boys, and complaining about all the stupid homework we were forced to complete by teachers who didn't know half as much as we did, or so we thought.

It was rare when we had time to talk. Andrew had long since left the commune, gone after that first summer. I felt that at least one of my prayers had been answered. His family needed his help, and even though his father had beaten the odds and had fully recovered from the farm accident, there was no reason for Andrew to remain with his Aunt and Uncle. I was elated when he left.

By the time Destiny and I were in our last year of high school, she had joined every social club on campus, reigned as Homecoming Queen – twice - and been the most sought after date for the Christmas Belle Formal and Senior Dance. As a junior, she had been invited by an older boy, the captain of the football team, and in her senior year, it seemed like the whole football team was waiting to take her to that once in a lifetime memory called prom.

Destiny wasn't fast or loose. In fact, she was still a virgin, determined to stay so until she married. But she was the most beautiful girl in school, as well as friendly, happy, and gregarious. Just the type you love to hate because you can't find one thing wrong with her, and certainly nothing to dislike.

I, on the other hand, stuck to my books, made a few friends who were outliers in the school social scene like me, grew three more inches, and lost twenty pounds. There were times when boys would stop in the hall and stare, but I always felt it was because I had something stuck in my teeth, or I was dragging around a piece of toilet paper stuck to my shoe. No one ever called me beautiful or singled me out for the girl they wanted to take anywhere, let alone to a school dance. I set my sights on the University of San Francisco. With early acceptance, I took the last two months of high school to relax. I still didn't know what Destiny had in mind past graduation day.

"I hadn't really thought about it, up until a few months ago. My mind was never on studies, like you, Rose. I guess I always thought my life would take care of itself, and I wouldn't have to do much more than be nice to get ahead."

"Didn't Uncle Jacob or Aunt Fern ever insist you take college entrance exams? You happy here? Thinking of staying?"

"Well, it's not so bad. I have a lot of friends from town and some are staying behind. They're not going straight off to college."

Destiny looked unsure of herself for the first time in her life. I thought she might feel some regret at not pursuing a college prep curriculum in favor of being popular and well liked. I felt grateful for my plain looks and the fact that I might actually escape the penned up life in the commune.

"It's always been so easy for you, Des, getting everything you ever needed or wanted simply by the way you looked. Oh, don't get me wrong, it's not your fault you were born beautiful." I glanced over to see if I could determine her reaction, which was more of surprise than the nod of affirmation I expected.

A look of incredulity washed across her face, and she threw up her hands in exasperation. She stopped short of taking the first bite of an apple and dropped it into her lap. "Are you kidding me?"

If I hadn't known better, I would have said Destiny was angry, even though I had never seen that side of her. She cocked her head in my direction and spoke in a decibel slightly higher than normal. "Do you think being told I was beautiful did me any favors?"

We hadn't talked in a long time. Certainly not on this topic. "You were so in love with Andrew when we were in middle school, you decided then and there your social life was over! You never flirted, dressed for attention, or even smiled much. You practiced looking unfriendly. And what did it get you? Have much fun? So, you got into the college of your choice. You probably would have done that anyway, you're so damn smart, but did you have any fun?" Destiny looked me up and down and shook her head, "And in case no one ever told you this before, you're the gorgeous one! I mean, look at you!"

I stiffened, sure she couldn't be talking about me. "Who? What? Me?"

"What question do you want me to answer first? You have it all, Rose. Brains, beauty, and now a way out of the commune and the promise of a bright future. Too bad you squandered all of high school thinking about that cousin of mine, and oh yeah....the idea that maybe, just maybe, River was not your father."

I blinked in surprise. "I don't remember ever talking about that with you. Not with anyone."

"You didn't. Your journal was open on your desk one day and I saw what you wrote. We were fifteen, maybe sixteen. That's an absurd idea, and I don't know where it came from. Do you really think someone else is your father? Is this what you spent the last three years thinking about?"

At that moment, I really looked at Destiny, delicate, raven-haired, face flushed with the tongue lashing she had just doled out on her best friend. I knew she was probably right. Just because I didn't have blue eyes like my parents didn't mean River was not my father. I looked at Destiny in earnest, and I knew for a fact WE looked nothing alike, so we could hardly be half-sisters. It was irrational and I was wasting too much time thinking about something, trying to prove something, that didn't need any proof at all.

I stammered, "I don't think about it all the time. You're right, it's illogical. A childish flight of fancy."

As far as Destiny was concerned, I let the matter drop for good. But even with the best of intentions to cease my mind from wandering in that direction, I still felt there was more to learn.

CHAPTER 9

Dressed for the arrival of warm weather in early June, Destiny looked like she stepped off the cover of Seventeen Magazine in her cut-off shorts and peasant top, riding just shy of her waistband. Our parents gave up long ago admonishing our chosen style of clothes, but mostly it was Destiny who caused them concern. She loved her body, and she intended to show it off.

On the cusp of adulthood, but feeling more like little girls, we wandered through the acreage of our property and spotted a cool patch amongst the trees in the peach orchard. The air was scented with the first burst of summer fruit, and we lounged and talked until sunset.

"Will you show me some make-up tricks? Go to Goodwill with me before I leave? There's gotta be a few fashionable pieces to choose from. You always find something stylish in a sea of cast-offs."

I admired Destiny as she stretched out on the blanket we had brought with us to cover the dry patches of leaves and dirt beneath the trees. *How do you always manage to look so marvelous, so fresh, with the hand-me-downs we have to choose from? I guess it's in your genes.*

"You're gonna have to get used to being beautiful one of these days, Rose." Destiny's eyes lit up. We were in her territory now. "I may as well be the one to make sure you never sell yourself short in the looks department. Boys will start to notice, you know."

With slightly curled lips, she shook her head slowly back and forth like she was talking to someone who didn't have the first clue about the opposite sex. She was right.

I COULDN'T WAIT TO LEAVE, earn a degree, and vowed I would never shop at another second-hand store as long as I lived. I knew I had to make my peace with Glory and River before exiting the commune. Their dream, not mine. I asked them more than once why they abandoned the comfort of their upper-class families in one of the most exciting cities in the world. Their answers always sounded vague, stressed they felt trapped, or there were too many rules, or society's values were corrupt, and they didn't want to raise their future children within the confines of a materialistic world. All gibberish to me, all platitudes of the hippie lifestyle. I convinced myself that the real reason was simmering just below the surface.

"I felt claustrophobic," Glory once said. "Too many people, too many rules, parents who couldn't see my point of view or share my values. I was going stir crazy."

Like I feel here in the commune. You ran from your comfortable upbringing, and I'm running right back to it. "I can hardly believe your lives were so awful that you chose to abandon all your opportunities, parents, family members, friends..."

Glory interrupted me, adamant and firm. It was unlike her to break into a conversation. "Didn't abandon our friends. They came with us. That's how we started out, a group of friends, like-minded, prepared to live off the land."

River sounded matter-of-fact. "Not so different from the path you're ready to take. Same as us." He looked lovingly at my mother, his Glory. His eyes darted in my direction as he took her hand and cradled it in his. "Children rarely follow in their parent's footsteps."

My parents knew from the beginning of my senior year that I would leave right after graduation. I made no secret of it, even though I eased into it slowly, left college brochures on the kitchen table, shared tidbits of information of what I hoped to become, what I wanted to study. Interior design dominated my dreams. Strange, since our furnishings were relics, my entire life consisted of old, used, discards, and I had never slept in a room where everything matched.

Maybe that's why I chose the field. Foreign, but desirable, perhaps it represented a way to make up for everything I thought I had missed out on in my childhood. It was a lofty goal in my mind, but I was ready to put in the work. I applied to a few colleges, mostly with the help of school counselors. River and Glory appeared disinterested, although they never discouraged me.

When the early acceptance letter from San Francisco State arrived in January of my senior year, I wanted nothing more than to wave it in their faces and shout at the top of my lungs, "I got accepted!"

Every time a classmate received an acceptance letter, they danced through the halls in celebration. I tempered my enthusiasm for just the right moment. I applied for various scholarships. Though awarded a partial one to cover books and tuition, I still needed funds for room and board. As far as I knew, there wasn't any extra cash laying around. I waited a week before approaching my mother.

"Glory, I have something to share and something to ask." River and Uncle Jacob had taken the day to go to the dump and forage through the discards and rejects in the hopes of finding some chairs to replace the tattered ones in our kitchen. Even my parents admitted they weren't worth saving, and we needed something new...dump new. I had my mother all to myself.

"Be right there, Rose. Would you mind clearing off the coffee table and adding some logs to the fire while I finish folding these clothes? I'll put on a fresh pot of coffee too. I don't think we've been alone like this in quite a while."

Glory made the best coffee. I took a liking to it as soon as I entered high school. It beat the drugs I suspected were passed around at weekend parties, those to which I was never invited. It turned out to be okay in some ways, because it kept me insulated, safe, and on track for what really mattered... college.

I heard in my mother's tone of voice how pleased she was that we had a few hours to ourselves. In front of the warm fire, sharing a freshly brewed pot of coffee, I suspected she would bring out the last two servings of peach cobbler, too. Time out during the day wasn't something we did often. I broke into a broad smile as I fluffed and arranged the pillows to cover the ancient stains on the cushions as I waited for my mother. I hoped she would see my point of view, unlike her own mother when she'd been my age, and offer to help.

"Just the two of us." Glory wrapped her delicate arms around my shoulders in an unexpected gesture of warmth after setting down steaming cups of coffee. She served them in two matching mugs I had picked up from a rummage sale years earlier when I was in grade school and bright colors still had some appeal. Hand-painted stoneware, they displayed orange and yellow daisies splashed on a white background.

They looked like they might have been part of a fine collection at one time, one of those sixty-piece sets from a well-known department store, the Sears catalog, or a wish book filled with everything from toasters to washing machines. I couldn't imagine what anyone would do with that many dishes, but I supposed there would be matching serving platters, cereal bowls, and salad plates. Nothing we needed. Even for Sunday dinner when there were six of us, we each used one plate for everything. Somehow, our food fit and no one ever complained. One of the mugs was bright orange on the inside, the other a sunny yellow, and I didn't even mind they came to our table in used condition. I still loved those mugs, and I handed the yellow one to Glory. It was her favorite color.

We sat in silence for a long time, draining the last sip for the special mugs. I could tell my mother detected I had something on my mind. I finally blurted, "Glory, I have some really exciting news I've been wanting to share with you and River."

"Oh?" She looked up from her drink and wrapped her hands around the mug as if she needed something to cling to. *She couldn't be that oblivious.* But I kept talking so I wouldn't lose my courage. "College, Glory. San Francisco State. I got early acceptance." I pulled the neatly folded piece of paper, no longer in the envelope, out of my shirt pocket and handed it to Glory.

Her hands appeared to shake as she took it from me. She assured me they were not, she was only trying to keep them warm by caressing the hot cup of coffee, even though all the liquid had been drained long before. A tear escaped from her eye and rolled down her cheek. I didn't know if I should hug her, say something, or sit silently and wait for her to speak first.

Swiping her eyes with the back of her hand, she broke into a grin and wrapped her arms around my shoulders, pulling me close. She whispered, "My Rose, I am so proud of you. I received early acceptance from San Francisco State when I was your age. I let it slip away. I chose another, safer path for myself. We started this commune. I don't regret it, but deep down I always wanted more for you."

"So you're not mad?"

"Why would I be mad?"

"Do you think River will be upset?"

"Why would your father be upset? We're intelligent people, Rose, just made different choices. We always wanted you to decide your own path. I guess we never felt it was important to tell you or say it out loud. We just figured you would know. And look what you did, on your own. I'm so proud of you, Rose." She beamed. It was the one reaction I never expected.

CHAPTER 10

I thought it interesting that Glory never asked how I planned to pay for my college education and River never brought it up. I guess my mother didn't share everything with him, and I didn't want to ruin the glow she was wearing or tarnish the rare mother-daughter moment we had shared.

"Rose, do you have a moment?"

I pushed shoes and boots out of the way that made it harder than normal to bypass the heap. Winter downpours saturated the ground, one storm in particular almost tearing off the roof. Rain boots, down jackets, and wet towels were wedged between the threshold and the porch to keep water from seeping under the door. I kicked a path to the living room as I peeled off my wet jacket and lace-up boots.

"Of course, I do. Now?"

"Now would be good. Coffee's on."

My body tensed, hoping for no bad news.

"Sit." Glory motioned to the couch. She had already arranged the pillows and cleared the coffee table of the piles of paper and envelopes that grew with every mail delivery. She didn't seem upset or sad, but I still braced myself.

"I bet you think I wasn't listening or cared when you told me about your acceptance to San Francisco State. I needed to talk to your father first. It took him awhile to agree and see the logic."

She poured the coffee from the carafe into my two favorite mugs. I could tell she had prepared the scene.

"I wasn't sure why River didn't say anything to me. I tried to handle everything myself. Scholarships, tuition, room and board. It's a lot. Counselors at school have been trying to help."

"Now they don't have to." Glory removed a letter from the pocket of her apron and slowly opened it. The corners of her mouth turned upward, a wide smile emerged, and I prepared myself to hear something good.

"I never went to college. Not because I couldn't get accepted or pay for tuition. My parents had started a college fund for me when I was born. Both of them threw it in my face the day I left home, and conversations between my mother and I have been scarce ever since."

I thought I detected a change in Glory's facial expression. My scalp started to tingle as I realized my mother was about to go somewhere that conjured up less than pleasant memories for her. She took a deep breath before reading the letter.

"I'm just going to read this letter I received from your grandmother the other day in response to the one I had written her. No need to go into too much detail."

I sank deep into the fluffed pillows behind my back, pulled my knees up to my chin, and wrapped my hands around the steaming mug of coffee to thaw my hands and still my pounding heart. My mother began.

My Dearest Daughter,

I must admit I was surprised to hear from you after all these years. We haven't talked in over a decade, and I haven't seen Rose since the Christmas before your father passed away. My, how time flies, as you are writing me about her acceptance to San Francisco State. What a coincidence. Was she aware that you had been accepted there, as well?

I can understand your dilemma, with little means to ensure her ability to actually attend in the fall. I hope you and River have been happy staying off life's grid, and you say you are. Believe it or not, I am happy for you.

I started to fidget and held my breath. I tried to relax. Glory's eyes didn't leave the page.

As for your questions about your college fund, I had totally forgotten about it until I received your letter. I was in such a state when I found out that your father never confided in me about our finances. If it hadn't been for his life insurance policy, I would not have been able to get by all these years. I've managed to live on very little, but I have everything I need. I checked with my bank the other day, and the account which held ten thousand dollars the day you and River left has grown handsomely over the years to almost fifty thousand dollars! I imagine you are as surprised as I was.

I blinked and held perfectly still as Glory continued. She trembled and her voice cracked as she turned over to the last page of the letter. I bit my lip until I tasted blood. The coffee had cooled to room temperature, but I took another sip.

There should be enough for four years room and board, books, and clothes if she is still able to take advantage of the partial scholarships offered by the University. Let me know when we can meet, and I will send plane fare for you, River, and Rose. I look forward to seeing all of you again. Know you have always had my heart.

Love,

Mother

"CAN I JUST SIT HERE for a moment?" I felt dumbfounded after listening to my mother read the letter from my grandmother. I could tell Glory was pleased, more than likely ecstatic, that she was able to share this kind of news with me after living off the land, providing me with nothing but hand-me-downs my entire life, and acting as though acquiring next to nothing was perfectly fine with her. I began to wonder if she ever regretted giving up her life in San Francisco, her comfortable surroundings for the meager existence she used as a replacement, or maybe it was an excuse for something else.

Don't go there, Rose. Enjoy the moment.

When I finally found my voice, I blurted out, "I'm speechless." I took Glory's hand. "I'm happy beyond words. I'm relieved." I inched closer to my mother and curled up in her arms. "I'm so thankful you did this for me. I know how hard it must have been for you."

"I would do anything for you, Rose. I knew you needed this. I've known since you were a little girl that our lifestyle was not the one cut out for you. But look at what you've accomplished on your own to make your future come true. You will be a force to be reckoned with, and I couldn't be...no make that we... couldn't be any prouder of our Rose."

We finished our coffee in silence. I let my imagination run wild. There would be other like-minded college students, late study nights, existential conversation, maybe a few dances and boys, but nothing was as heartening as thinking about my freedom. At long last. When River came barging into the room, dripping wet and shaking off the rain, he could tell Glory and I had been talking. There was no mistaking the calm, and he sensed the mood in the room.

"I see two very happy women, my girls, sitting on the couch without speaking," he said, "but I hear volumes. Everything all right?"

He stepped over the mound of jackets and boots as I had done earlier and shed his outer layer. What came next was a bit of a surprise, but a welcome one. Without saying a word, he bent over me, kissed me on the forehead and cradled my face in his hands. "Love you, Rose. You're a good girl." He winked at Glory as he passed by and went in search of something dry to wear.

I couldn't recall a time when I'd felt this happy, and I never wanted the feeling to end.

CHAPTER 11

It was the beginning of September and San Francisco was unpleasantly hot. I had expected drizzle and fog. Instead, I encountered a stifling dorm room on the 4th floor, no air conditioning, sweaty bodies roaming from one end of the hall to the other, and a roommate who had already staked her claim on the bed closest to the window, secured and fastened to prevent the flow of fresh air. The best I could do upon entering was to open it as far as it would go in order to attract some type of circulation in the oppressive heat. I was met with a surprised look as my roommate retraced my steps and tightly shut it again.

"Too much breeze." She pulled her hair tight to one side as if to keep it in the perfect shape it had been styled, complicated looking and really not all that attractive. I would have thought the layers of hair spray could control anything, even in a monsoon. "My hair is getting all blown around and loose papers are all over the place." She was abrupt and didn't bother to look at me as she spoke. I thought about responding in an equally unfriendly tone, but let the matter drop. There were higher priorities on my list.

I had noticed a few bits and pieces of paper starting to

blow, but her hair, even though not styled to my taste, still looked better than mine. Too hot to do anything but pull it back in a ponytail, it remained scraggly from the humidity with uncontrollable wisps of hair that poked out in every direction. I probably looked like a mess to her, but it was comfortable for me. I envisioned a long semester with a spoiled only child, no experience in sharing, and frequent demands to get her way, no matter the cost.

I plopped my gently used, second-hand duffle bag on the hard, narrow mattress and looked around for a spot to sit.

"Oh, okay. I'm sure I can cool off in the common lounge down the hall if it gets too oppressive. I think I noticed a water cooler in the corner. But could we open the window? A crack?" I motioned with my fingers, pinching them together with a gap no wider than an inch. It's getting hard to breathe. We can put a book on the stack of papers, like a paperweight. That should take care of that problem for the moment."

I noticed her name, Cecily Monroe, on a placard, eye level, outside our door. My name was underneath, pecking order already established. I sucked it up. This girl and I would be sharing close quarters for at least six months.

"Hi, Cecily. Pretty name. My name is Rose."

"Sorry for the opening introduction, Rose. I wanted to get settled before you arrived so you could have some room to arrange your belongings. It's so tight in here. I'm not used to being this cramped. I spent two hours on my hair this morning before my parents drove me in from the city." She took a brief look in the mirror, checking sideways, front ways, craning to see her coif from the back. "A lot of good it did me."

Cecily's face opened up with a self-deprecating smile, and I relaxed. I decided to give her a break. I decided to give myself a break. We were all new, on our own for the first time. Maybe it won't be such a long semester after all, I thought. And hoped.

"Do you mind if we start over?"

I did another quick overview of the room, dropped my defenses, and complimented her on her fluffy bedspread, pillows, and what looked like her favorite stuffed animal from her childhood. A little frilly for my tastes, I couldn't handle pink. I knew her in an instant. We had nothing in common, but I actually was grateful for her head start. I took the next hour to get myself settled. I wasn't looking forward to unpacking my dreadful bedspread, second hand, of course. Grandmother said she would buy me anything I needed, but I was determined to use what my mother had lovingly packed for me, instead. It would kill Glory if she knew I was less than pleased with the extra effort she made to find the right freshman decor from Goodwill for my dorm room. I needed to look at the big picture.

"Thanks for arriving early." I moved towards the door so Cecily would follow my lead. Gripping the handle as she passed through the threshold, I said, "I like your hair." I lied.

WE STROLLED TOGETHER down the corridor, acclimating ourselves to the environs of dorm living. It would be loud, for sure. Freshmen, sophomores, a few juniors arrived in all shapes and sizes. Most of the girls looked fresh out of high school, and they probably felt as lost as we did. Some had already situated themselves in front of the TV set in the common area. Others took advantage of their last weekend of summer, checking out the activity board and bolting for the front door.

I marveled at the momentum and excitement that permeated the air and took a deep breath to still my thoughts. *Had I been too hasty with my decision to leave the commune? Did my school girl fantasy of trying to come to grips with my parentage propel me into an environment where I didn't belong?*

I shrugged it off. I knew I had made the right decision.

Cecily and I continued to investigate our surroundings.

Almost in passing, more of a question to myself than to Cecily, I asked," What do you think I would look like with short hair?"

I pulled at the uncombed ends, a head of hair that hadn't been trimmed in a decade and had absolutely no style. It was just hair, lots of it, lackluster, drab, and long, in need of something different to coincide with my long-awaited sense of freedom...a more mature, post-high school appearance.

"I think you would look adorable. Open your face. People could see your eyes. They're really pretty, Rose...so dark...very unusual."

I startled. *Nice of her to say.*

I tried to imagine myself with hair that didn't go past my waist. A short pixie – no, too drastic. Maybe a perm – not even my most rebellious self could justify a move that extreme.

The next morning I found a hairdresser close to campus, a wise choice I thought, since there was a line out the door by the time I arrived without an appointment. She convinced me that a blunt cut, shoulder length, feathered bangs, a slight undercut to create movement was what my perfect oval face needed.

I reluctantly followed her advice. I winced when she pulled all my hair away from my face, tied it loosely with a rubber band, and with one motion of her razor-sharp scissors, sheared off the entire mass of hair three inches below the knot. I could hear it sever every strand, like slicing bread, and watched it fall at my feet in a dull brown heap, ready to be swept up and thrown in the trash. Almost two decades of my identity, in five seconds, gone.

My face registered my shock and horror. I felt the chair slowly turn around, my back to the mirror, as the stylist prepared herself to take on the challenge. After what felt like hours, she finally removed the black cape, shook off the pieces of uneven, chopped waves and tendrils that clung to the plastic, and gently rotated the seat to reveal my image. Pleased with herself and waiting for my reaction, I squeezed my eyes shut. I was unsure if I might cry at the end result, a vision so unfamiliar, I was positive I would hate it. I regretted taking the plunge, and before I peered out from my new, shagged bangs brushed to the side just below my eyebrows, I held my breath and reassured myself that it was just hair. If I didn't like it, even if I detested it or was embarrassed by it, it would always grow back. I took a deep breath and opened my eyes.

I followed my reflection in every store window all the way home. A few boys, ready to pursue conquests and casual victories, cast second glances in my direction. A totally new experience for me. I put my head down and walked quickly past, too fearful to engage in conversation or to stop to get acquainted, but by the time I reached my room, my confidence had soared.

"So cute!" shrieked Cecily when I flung open the door and presented myself to the only person who had seen both the before and after version of me.

CHAPTER 12

Most weekends I had the room to myself. Cecily and I got along well enough during the week, but she preferred the spaciousness of her parent's home to the cramped quarters and rowdiness of dorm life. Her home was not more than an hour's drive from campus, and she looked for any excuse to invite three or four of her girlfriends to join her. Not me, though. She found her own group and I did the same, but our individual routines worked for both of us. She once told me she was only in school to find a rich husband. I, on the other hand, was only in school to find a career. Marriage? I hadn't thought that far ahead yet. I had work to do and kept my eye on the prize. That is until one night in late winter, the first night of a three-day weekend. I was invited to a bonfire at Ocean Beach.

It was a favorite hangout for college students, the longest and widest beach in San Francisco and never crowded. The sand stretched along the length of the coast for over three miles, unspoiled and untouched – miles of sand and water as far as the eye could see. I joined the other revelers after sunset, flames from the bonfire already curling up into the black February sky. They created a surreal backdrop to the sounds of crashing waves, not all that distant since the tide was high, and daring frat boys continued to challenge one another to dive into the frigid water.

I was not accustomed to out-of-control, rambunctious crowds and thought about leaving before I even had a chance to search the landscape for someone I knew. I spied a girl from my Art History class and waved frantically to get her attention.

"Thank God," we said in unison.

Relieved to find each other, we staked out a spot just outside the warmth of the fire ring. Beach blankets were strewn in a haphazard array, a welcome invitation to anyone who wanted to sit instead of stand, a perfect landing for an observer like myself.

Music blared and beer and wine coolers were passed around like water. I thought that if my parents had ever done anything like this in their youth, I'd never heard about it. They had never shared their teenage memories with me.

Relax, Rose. Take a deep breath and enjoy yourself.

It had been a long four months, and I had studied until my eyes burned from too little sleep and my fingers felt blistered from pounding all day and night on my typewriter. I completed my first semester with almost perfect grades, save Chemistry. Science was always a mystery to me and, except for satisfying a GE requirement, I had no interest in pursuing additional courses in anything scientific.

My Grandmother had made vague suggestions about how nice it would be if I became a doctor or lawyer, aspirations I'm sure she had at one time for Glory. I side-stepped the conversation and steered it in another direction. I wasn't interested in pinning myself down just yet with a major, but so far, I still clung to the idea that I was meant to be an interior designer, have a fabulous and enticing career in the City, and make a lot of money.

I felt a tap on my shoulder, soft, almost indiscernible. I thought to myself before checking that it must have been a leaf or a sudden gust of wind. I turned my head and saw a beautiful young man, one I knew, one I had spent too many hours thinking about and wishing he had noticed me. Wasted years.

Stay calm.

"Rose, it's been a long time. I hardly recognized you." He shifted his stance, backed up, and put space between us.

I struggled to assess the situation and couldn't help but notice his hair was longer. It gave him an apostolic quality that heightened his masculinity instead of stripping it. The last time I saw him, he still had the rangy, undeveloped quality of a high school boy. Now, I was looking at a man...an exquisitely handsome, drop-dead gorgeous man.

I twirled the ends of my hair between my thumb and forefinger, self-conscious about the length. I suddenly regretted abandoning my childhood tresses for a more grown-up style.

Should I give him a smile, a hug, a shrug? Whatever you do, make it casual. My heart raced. *Why does this person have this kind of power over me?*

"Oh, my! It's you! It's Andrew!"

That's all that came out of my mouth, pathetic words from someone who was never at a loss for stringing together sentences and conversing on a mature level. I had spent years thinking about what I might say if I ever saw him again, and those were the only words my mind would produce. He smiled, and I hope he could sense how awkward I felt.

"Yup, it's me. I almost didn't recognize you. You've gotten taller and you cut your hair." Andrew started to stammer. It was his turn to feel uncomfortable. "But...you look great...I mean I like it short. Looks very collegiate....did I just say that?"

He seemed as nervous as I felt, which caught me off-guard. I wanted to respond and tell him that he was still the most gorgeous man I had ever met, and I didn't think I would ever date another soul because he ruined it for me before I was a freshman in high school. But four years had helped me develop a filter, and I kept my thoughts to myself. Instead, I blurted, "Well, you haven't changed a bit. You look great, too."

"There are two empty chairs by the bonfire and so far no one has claimed them. Shall we?" He waited for my answer. I had no time to rehearse a response, even though I had imagined this conversation in my head a hundred times. My mind went blank.

"I mean, if you want to. I'd love to catch up and find out how your family is doing. Destiny...River and Glory. You don't have to...."

I turned to my girlfriend, my eyebrows raised in a silent question mark. She smiled and waved the two of us off in the direction of the fire pit.

I found my voice. "No, that sounds great. Why don't I grab them before anyone else and you can get us something to drink?"

"Beer okay?"

I hardly ever drank. I thought it might help if I had a little something to calm my nerves. "Sounds perfect."

I felt light-headed and more alive than I had since leaving home and as I removed my tennis shoes and dragged my bare feet through the cold sand, every sense within me burst to life. The dancing flames of the bonfire burned brighter, the laughter of the crowd sounded more cheerful, the waves exuded a fragrant aroma of salty air, and the night sky was covered with a blanket of stars. I felt thrust into a scene I had only fantasized about. It was too good to be true. I forced my mind not to wander.

I SHOULD FEEL REMORSEFUL, I should feel ashamed of myself. Those were my first thoughts as I awakened to the soft rain that pelted the window. I hoped it wasn't a dream and slowly opened my eyes.

Andrew's lanky body took up most of my twin size mattress, meant for one and comfortable for none. I lay there, entranced with his masculine beauty, the strength of his shoulders, the perfect way his sandy blonde hair parted to one side and fell effortlessly into place on the pillow, and the smooth, chiseled chest that was certainly the result of a childhood on the farm.

He was sound asleep, and I watched him breathe like it was a movie, afraid to move and envision the credits rolling... "The End."

I didn't want it to be over. I stretched my arms behind my head, careful not to wake him from his restful slumber. I had no idea what would come next. This moment was mine to savor. In the silence, I felt his body move and adjust slightly to the cramped arrangement as he reached out for me in the dark.

He encircled me with his muscular arms and mumbled the sweetest sound, "Good Morning, my sweet Rose," and we were one again.

By the time we stumbled out of bed, we could hear raucous laughter in the hallways and the sudden chaos of college students on the loose for the weekend.

"I guess we'd better get dressed," Andrew said casually. He threw my sweatshirt and Levis, crumpled in a heap on the floor from the night before, in my direction. "Come on, let's grab some breakfast. I'm starved."

What was a monumental moment to me seemed like a casual encounter, practiced and routine, to Andrew. I pulled myself to the edge of the bed and made a bold move. I didn't want breakfast. I didn't want anything more to do with this fantasy if I couldn't wrap my head around what had happened and determine if this was the perfect beginning, or an unceremonious ending.

Be careful, don't sound hurt or demanding. Say something to get a clue. Listen for a clue, a tone, a word. "Did you know I had a crush on you in middle school?"

I scrambled to find my shoes and a clean pair of socks from my one and only drawer, careful not to look at him. I wanted the comment to sound off-handed, while giving him an opportunity to respond. My purity had been given willingly, a fact of which he was aware. While I assured myself it probably meant more to me than it did to him, I wanted him to know without actually saying it, that what we shared was important for me. I sensed that, with his confidence and good looks, he was well beyond me in experience. My mind raced and my heart beat faster as I conjured up dozens of girlfriends who had come before this night - my night - with Andrew.

I startled when he moved closer and pulled me up from the bed, one sock still dangling from my trembling hand. He bent over to whisper softly in my ear, "You're the first, Rose."

Both of us stood there, waiting for the other to say something, but nothing came out of either one of us. Instead, we wrapped our arms around each other and held on tight, until the moment was shattered by a skirmish outside the door. It reminded us that we were on our way to breakfast. The weekend had begun.

There's your clue, Rose. And make a note, he's a man of few words.

CHAPTER 13

The second half of the year flew by, while I felt like I was floating on air. Nothing bothered me and nothing could dampen my spirits - not even the never-ending assignments and term papers, early morning classes or late night cram sessions.

My imagination picked up where our moments together left off. I caught myself more than once in the middle of a lecture hall, jolted back to reality by a professor determined to keep everyone's attention by pounding his fist on the podium when he wanted to make a point. American History always seemed to have a point. My head was filled with days and nights with Andrew, our hopes, our dreams, and our ambitions. We also unlocked a brazen appetite for the flesh as we memorized every curve of our bodies during stolen, breathless moments.

We raced towards the finish line together of completing our second semesters, closer to our degrees which seemed the natural order of things. Andrew, two years ahead of me, aimed towards a degree in Architecture. He felt certain he would land a job in one of the many firms throughout the San Francisco Bay area. Building was burgeoning, and he had an eye for style and state-of-the-art projects that rose as quickly as the cost of living.

I held tight to my chosen major of interior design, eager to put formal education behind me and capture the world. I was no longer interested in obtaining an advanced degree. Too many years spent with my nose in books already. Now, I could shave at least three years off of my education. Even though River and Glory let me make my own decisions and never interfered, Grandmother made no secret of her disappointment. She wanted to see me take my education as far as I could, BA, Masters, PhD. She wanted it all for me, but I didn't want it for myself.

Summer loomed. What weary college student, after two weeks of studying for finals and suffering sleepless nights that derailed us from all civility, doesn't welcome the freedom of summer and the long forgotten delight of languishing in bed until noon?

I dreaded it, uncertain if these last few months with Andrew would end up being nothing more than a filler for extra-curricular activities or if we really had a future. Parting, even for a short period of time, made me feel like our connection would disintegrate, our relationship would never survive the separation, and he would find someone new if I let him out of my sight.

We talked about living arrangements. Should we find something together off campus and move in together? Was the timing right? Could I stay with Grandmother, then return to River and Glory? Andrew's family begged him to come home for a few months. They saw him slipping into his adult life as they lost their grip on their eldest child.

Finally, it boiled down to what neither of us wanted, but what we both felt was necessary in order to please our families. We would separate, take a break from one another for the summer, and return to school together in the fall.

I made plans to travel to the Pacific Northwest to spend time with Glory and River, but not before spending a lazy week in the city with my grandmother. She had promised to bring out old photo albums and share a glimpse of my mother's childhood.

"Not as unpleasant as she might want you to believe, my dear. And you are more like her than you want to admit." I pondered her words often and I began to look forward to a week with her alone, no homework, no company, just the two of us.

Andrew, though not eager, planned to spend the summer with his parents and two younger sisters. The years he spent helping his father during his recovery and being a crutch for his mother turned him into a man, a responsible man. Any woman would be lucky to marry him. I spent far too many of my waking hours daydreaming that I would be the lucky one.

"It won't be too bad, my love." Andrew started calling me that after our first breakfast together. "Don't be shocked," he told me off-handedly. "I've never felt like this before and I don't have to spend time contemplating words of endearment. You're my love, Rose."

"So what am I supposed to call you?" I smiled, thinking of all the sugar-coated words people often called one another.

"I'm sure something will come to you. Don't make a big deal out of it, my love." He winked, that sexy, meant only for me, delightful wink.

I still hadn't coined that magical phrase, title, term. *Andy* was definitely not in the running. Neither was *Babe* or *My Man*. Andrew was right. It would come to me. I had all summer to think about it.

"So, this is it until the fall, my love." Andrew descended the front steps of my dormitory, carrying the last of my belongings in his arms as we walked slowly to my car, a 1990 burgundy Ford Taurus.

The color was hideous. I cringed every time I approached, but it was a reasonable purchase for a well-tuned, functional vehicle. It was far better than my grandmother's first suggestion when she told me that Glory's 1975 baby blue Pinto, still unblemished with less than 5,000 miles on the odometer, was all mine if I wanted it. I had heard too many horror stories about this vehicle and felt queasy at the thought that my mother had once driven it, unaware that it would one day carry the nickname, 'car bomb.' Fuel tanks erupted in flames with rear-end collisions and damaging PR reports dogged the automaker for decades.

"Oh, Grandmother, I don't know about that. If it hasn't been driven all these years, it might need a lot of repairs." I hoped she would get the hint. She was offering me a precious keepsake in her mind. To me, the embarrassment would far outweigh the sentiment. "Where is it, anyway?"

"In storage. I've had it in storage all these years. An old family friend. Well, a good friend of your grandfather's. Maybe he owed him a favor, maybe he felt sorry for me after he died. I'm sure he would love to get it out of his garage."

Her eyes lit up, a smile appeared, the kind you get when lost in thought or recalling a particular, priceless moment in time. I never doubted her intention, thinking she could pass it down to me, a continuation of the past that had been abruptly interrupted with my mother's departure from her life. It had pained me to reject her offer. Grandmother got a good deal on the trade-in and I had nothing to complain about.

"This is hard. I don't want to say good-bye." I could hear

myself whining as I clutched Andrew's arm and practically knocked him over while he tried to balance the last box in the back seat.

"It's only a couple months. Enjoy your family. Enjoy Destiny. Enjoy yourself." He had a way of making me feel warm, protected and cared for just by smiling at me.

"You're right." I grabbed his face for one last kiss, then poured myself into the driver's seat, the only empty space, the rest of the car overloaded with material possessions I hadn't even realized until then that I had collected. "See you in a couple months. Call me, write me, *visit me?* Until next fall then....handsome." And there it was. I said the word, and it sounded right. Handsome.

He grinned at me. "What happens when I'm eighty years old, and I'm not so handsome anymore?" He burst into laughter and then hugged me so hard, I fought for breath. He looked very pleased.

"You will always be handsome to me." My heart fluttered...eighty years old...I didn't have anything to worry about.

"Okay, we'll see, my love."

We disengaged from one last passionate kiss. Then, I watched him walk away towards his own dorm to collect his belongings. I put the car in gear and pulled into traffic.

CHAPTER 14

Andrew and I kept our love affair under a veil of secrecy, deciding it would be better to discuss our budding romance with our parents in person. I think Grandmother had an inkling. She once asked me if I had a boyfriend, but I ignored her question and changed the subject. But she knew. Elderly people always seem to know when something is not quite as it seems. I suppose age brings not only wisdom, but an uncanny ability to read between the lines and peer into the soul. I didn't want to be old anytime soon, but I considered how liberating it would be to move through every-day life so fluidly, cut to the chase, and take emotion down to a reasonable level.

As much as I wanted to get to Grandmother's, I decided on a slight detour first. I changed my route as the thought of living with Andrew when we returned to school in the fall started to percolate in my mind. We hadn't even looked at neighborhoods or thought about how we would pay rent, but I took myself on a flight of fancy through some affordable areas. It could work. Maybe Grandmother would allow me to use the money she provided for room and board to my portion of rent, but living together would probably be too far out of her realm of what was proper for a young lady.

The fog began to roll in, and I knew delaying my arrival at grandmother's home wouldn't make me miss Andrew any less. I cut short my self-guided tour of college student filled apartment houses by the university and looked for the next entrance onto the freeway. I was a pretty good driver, having mastered a stick shift and parallel parking on the old truck at the commune. Still, I dreaded the drive into the city and the cramped streets, steep inclines, and lousy parking options in Grandmother's neighborhood.

There was no such thing as a garage in those old Victorian homes and finding a nearby, open space on the street always proved to be a problem. People who grew up there had long gotten used to the inconvenience, but occasional visitors like myself experienced frustration and annoyance. It would be my luck that I would have to heave my belongings two blocks, if I was lucky enough to find a space at all.

As I turned the corner to the now familiar street, perched at the top of a steep decline into the city below, my breath suddenly stilled at the spectacular panoramic view before me. Even though the day had turned dull and the mist hovered over the Golden Gate Bridge, I was surrounded by brilliant architecture in every direction. Dozens of charming Victorian homes, the painted ladies, lined the streets in both directions, punctuated by corner markets and one-of-a-kind specialty shops. It was a testament to the influence on the history of California and the discerning eye of the builders who prompted the city's growth. No wonder Andrew had chosen this ambition for his life's work. I caught myself thinking about a wedding, then a sweet little first apartment, then one child, making our cramped quarters impossible for a growing family, then a move to the suburbs, neighborhood barbeques, another child, two cars....my mind raced and the light turned green.

My fantasy warmed me. I could physically feel joy in the pit of my stomach. I asked Destiny once, after we had gotten an almost-new pair of identical boots from the thrift store as a special treat before we started third grade, "Do you feel that, Des?"

"Feel what?" She hadn't the vaguest idea of what I meant.

"That dancing in your tummy, silly! It's like your insides are giggling."

It felt delicious to me and ever since that time, a happy moment or extraordinary event could trigger my sense of well-being. My whole body would tingle with pleasure and delight with that feeling of joy.

I didn't mind driving around the block four times before I found a place to park. I grabbed one suitcase, my wallet, keys, and bounded up Grandmother's stairs, only slightly winded from the short sprint. I met her at the door with a huge grin, amused at my own story of happily ever after.

"You look flushed, Rose. Did you run all the way here?"

"I didn't notice. I do feel a little warm, but I think I'm just excited to have finals over, spend the summer with Glory and River, and take a week off with you to do whatever we want. I'm excited about seeing Destiny, too. It's been almost a year. I had to miss her wedding, because she planned it right in the middle of winter mid-terms, and her first baby is the end of summer."

"Well, first things first."

What did that mean? First things first? I was starting to see how generations change, each subsequent one holding on to the popular expressions that conveyed their thoughts. What was first to Grandmother was most likely not what was first to me, which was kicking off my shoes and checking the refrigerator for a Dr. Pepper.

"Yes, Grandmother, first things first."

"Take off your coat and hang it on the hall tree. Your room is ready, so you can take your suitcase upstairs. Then, come on down and get yourself a cold drink. I got plenty of Dr. Pepper just for you."

I smiled. We weren't that far apart after all.

MY GRANDMOTHER WAS PRETTY easy to get along with, but hard to understand. I couldn't quite grasp the fact that she effortlessly embraced my presence, yet she kept her distance from her own daughter. Nobody ever said anything. No one offered any explanations, which intrigued me even more when my mind drifted back to our dinner table with Uncle Jacob and my father.

Even as a child, I felt they were a little too close, but maybe I just didn't value the idea of communal living. I grabbed a Dr. Pepper from the well-stocked refrigerator and joined my grandmother on the outside veranda, two levels above the busy street below, and the perfect perch to thumb through the old memories.

A small woman, like all the other females in my family save myself, my grandmother stepped out to the porch, arms overflowing with tattered, leather-bound, photo albums. Some smelled like mothballs, but one in particular still contained the fragrant aroma of real leather, earthy and slightly sweet, a bronze label on the front engraved with the words, Caroline Nicole 1956 – 1974.

Not only was it in perfect condition, it almost looked like

it had gone untouched since the last picture was inserted between the pages. The stack of albums would take all afternoon to sort through, but I was only interested in one book.

"Here, Grandmother, let me help you with those." I balanced my Dr. Pepper on the railing and moved forward to lend a hand.

"That's sweet of you, Rose. They are a little bulky for this old woman to grip."

"I don't even know what's old anymore," I responded. "I'm about the same age Glory was when she left home, still a teenager, but in some ways I feel much older than that. When I was five or six, I remember playing with the other children in the commune, those who had already started learning multiplication and division. I thought they were so old and they were ten."

Grandmother and I both laughed as we made ourselves comfortable on the porch and spread the photos out before us.

I didn't hesitate or ask which one to examine first. My curiosity got the better of me as I grabbed the book with my mother's name. "Do you mind?"

"Of course, not. I'm not surprised you want to look at your mother's photos first."

The leather had become stiff from years of sitting on a shelf, and the binding cracked when I slowly turned back the cover. For the time, this must have been an expensive album, not like the ones from the dime store that had puppies or horses on the cover and a sheet of plastic you could pull back to secure the pictures. Eventually, they fell apart, the slightly sticky surface began to crumble, and most of them came loose, lost their position, and fell out.

No, this album was meant to last a lifetime. It must have

been nice to have the means to acquire the finest things money could buy. I tried not to think about all my used belongings and the lack of anything new in our home when I was growing up.

My mother was a beautiful baby. I studied each and every picture that bore her image, from infancy to puberty, transfixed by one in particular. July 1956. My mother's newborn picture. She couldn't have been more than a week old. Grandmother cradled her in her arms, a radiant glow on her face that was hard to disguise. She was beautiful then, and I could see the resemblance between her and Glory right away.

Maybe the older we get, the more we look like our same gender parents. It sure seems like that anyway. My mother had the roundest, largest, deep blue eyes I had ever seen, and even though still as beautiful, they no longer stand out quite in the same way as they did on her baby face.

As I analyzed the photograph, I noticed a photo of a little boy on a small table beside my mother and grandmother. He looked to be about three years old. He stood on the top step of the front porch, the same place we were sitting.

It must have been 4th of July or Memorial Day, because he wore little blue shorts and a red and white striped t-shirt. Above the door hung an American Flag, and he held a smaller flag on a stick, smiling and grinning in an angelic moment captured by the camera.

I wasn't sure I should ask or question my grandmother about this surprising image of someone I never knew existed, but my imagination was running wild. I decided direct was best. "Who's the little boy? There, in the picture on the table." I pointed to the photo in the background of the photo of my newborn mother.

"You don't miss anything, do you, Rose? Your mother never told you?"

"Told me what?"

"That she had a brother. Or she would have if he had lived."

I thought then that I should have kept my mouth shut. I saw my grandmother's eyes turn sorrowful and distant. I knew what was coming next and my heart ached for her.

"No. She never said anything." I didn't have time to contemplate why Glory never mentioned a brother. I felt concerned for my grandmother and the grief I had resurrected. "What happened? Is it all right if I ask?"

"Certainly. You can ask me anything." She fumbled in her pocket for a hankie.

Women of a certain generation still used cloth hankies instead of disposable tissues. Grandmother had a stack of them on her dresser. I often watched her methodically iron, fold, and stack a month's worth of the pastel squares, frayed at the edges, but not ready for the trash.

"Waste not, want not." Grandmother uttered another of her often used phrases. I thought it sounded silly, but I still pondered her words and came to understand the values she was trying to impart. Hankies were used for blowing one's nose and crying, maybe both at the same time. I hoped I hadn't unleashed a river of tears or old memories I should have left alone.

"Jonathan. Jonathan Edward Morrison II. He was named after your grandfather, who hoped that one day there might be a Jonathan Edward Morrison III. Shortly after that photograph was taken in 1952, he contracted polio." Grandmother dabbed her cheek with her hankie. She appeared composed, but I saw her struggle to continue.

"You don't have to tell me any more. It's okay, grandmother." I wasn't sure if she could tell me the rest of the story without breaking down, and for all of my curiosity, I wasn't sure if I wanted to hear.

"I'm fine, really. You should know." She calmed herself, twisting the now damp handkerchief between her fingers, never letting go of the cloth that served as a visual for her broken heart. "It was the worst outbreak in our nation's history, and children were especially vulnerable. Over three thousand children died. Jonathan was one of them. He was barely four years old, and he was gone. Your grandfather was never the same, even after your mother was born. I'm not surprised she never told you. She never even met him, but his little ghost was everywhere. For most of her childhood, it was just the two of us. Her father traveled a lot and never again took comfort in our home or found peace with the family he created. He never got over losing his little boy."

Missing puzzle pieces - the ones that caused me to question why we never visited my mother's or my father's parents, the ones that created flights of fancy when I was bored or had nothing better to do, and the made up reasons why I was brought up on a commune instead of the warm environment of a multi-generational family were all starting to fall into place.

I was still inquisitive, but I made up my mind right then and there that, if I ever married and had children, they would know their grandparents. I would never deny children of mine the knowledge of where they came from or what my life had been like growing up...even if it was in a commune. I didn't know what to say to my grandmother, who sat beside me with a remote look on her face as she turned her head slightly to view the spot where her little boy stood the last time his image had been captured.

"They say time heals. It doesn't. Not really." She rested her hand on the precious image and caressed it softly as though he was a tangible presence, not simply a likeness of the flesh and blood toddler she once had cradled in her arms. "Life changes. New people can substitute for those we lost, but that unique space once filled by someone special will never be occupied by another. The deep void will remain for life."

I realized it was still there for my grandmother and probably was not the only one that created an emptiness in her heart.

I turned each page with a mix of reverence and awe, savoring the progression of my mother's childhood. Grandmother let out an occasional chuckle. In some instances, she sighed with resignation. My mother had been a beautiful child. I realized she never experienced an unattractive phase, unlike most of us. Destiny was like that, always the prettiest girl everywhere we went, never an ugly day, and certainly not an awkward year, or two, or three.

On the last page, I paused. A smiling Glory, surrounded by a group of friends in Golden Gate Park, birthday cake ablaze with candles, the message written in pink frosting, 'Happy 18th Birthday, Caroline.' Standing beside her, his hand resting gently on her arm, my mother's expression being one of taking that big breath just before the candles are blown out, was Uncle Jacob.

Aunt Fern stood to his other side, looking directly into the camera, a smile so big, she was probably the only one who listened to the photographer when he said, "Say Cheese!"

River was an accent in the background of familiar faces, hair down to his shoulders, a mustache that highlighted his good-looking, boyish appeal, a headband of Indian beads encircling his forehead. His eyes were trained on Glory as she took obvious pleasure in this celebration. I wondered what she could have been wishing for on that eighteenth birthday, exactly eight months before my birth.

I tried to act nonchalant and surprised. "Is that Uncle Jacob? Next to Glory?"

I wasn't sure who had taken the photograph or how it came to be in grandmother's possession, but she must have been familiar with my mother's friends.

"It sure is. His mother, Rose, and I had known each other since grade school, and he and your mother grew up together. Same grade school, middle school, high school. All the way through. They were best friends."

Grandmother was more animated than I had ever seen her, and she seemed to enjoy the memories resurrected from a long-forgotten past. "Anyway, Steven...I mean River. Guess that's what you call him. I couldn't get used to calling him by that name any more than I could call your mother Glory. He and Jacob met in high school, and they became inseparable. Played on the same sports teams, both excelled, both got accepted to good schools. That's how your mother and father were introduced...through Jacob." She rattled off the information, not a hint of sarcasm or prejudice in her tone.

"You said Uncle Jacob's mother was named Rose?"

Grandmother nodded.

I filed the information in my head since she didn't seem bothered or intrigued. The connection was not as obvious to her as it was to me.

"What about Aunt Fern? She hasn't changed much."

"Fern and Jacob started dating as sophomores, and she and your mother saw each other almost every day. The two couples were always together. Guess it made perfect sense for them to find a way of living that suited their dream to be in each other's lives, without the threat of losing touch or living in different states."

"And Glory was pregnant with me, right?" I kept my voice low and calm. "I'm not a child, I can see by the dates on the picture. I was born eight months after it was taken, and Destiny was also born around the same time. Did they both know they were pregnant when they all decided to leave and move to a commune?"

Grandmother took the book from my hands.

I discerned an undertone of hurt and anger, the glow from her kind and gentle face replaced by a dull, mournful expression. Even so, I pressed, "I don't get it. Is there something you're not telling me?"

I knew I crossed an invisible line. She pulled back, reluctant to share. It was the beginning of the unraveling, according to my Grandmother, but it was only one side of the story. I couldn't fathom why my parents would turn their backs on everything given to them, the upscale lifestyle, the opportunities reserved only for those lucky enough to be born into families of wealth. I didn't want to appear ungrateful to my grandmother. Maybe the topic would come up again during my visit, and then I could approach her...gently.

In a barely audible tone, she murmured, "You'll have to ask your parents."

Grandmother seemed unsure, uncomfortable, and no longer willing to engage. I changed the subject. Not that I wanted to. There were too many questions left unanswered, but the seed had been planted and my resolve to find the truth deepened. I tried to comprehend what grandmother had just told me.

Did she not realize I'd been named after Uncle Jacob's mother? That my mother was pregnant with me before she left San Francisco? What else was being hidden from me? Maybe I wasn't so far off after all with my wild imagination, especially when I pondered the idea of Uncle Jacob being my father.

I studied the photo in the album, quite possibly the last one grandmother ever took of Glory. I didn't want to share with her the suspicions I had harbored for so long. I set the book on top of the stack of photos yet to be discovered. She didn't sense my sudden change of demeanor. Just as well, since I didn't have any idea where to begin or how to process this new information.

CHAPTER 15

I took my time driving back home. Instead of taking the interstates, I chose to travel highways off the beaten path. I snaked through the coastal route, stopped for lunch at a roadside diner, and appreciated the landscape in its natural splendor. I needed two days for the long drive to our commune in Washington, and it provided me with time to reflect and understand the importance of my discovery.

Grandmother pressed a $100 bill into my hand, then kissed my cheek. "Please find a nice hotel to spend the night...half way...maybe just after you get into Oregon. Have a wonderful summer, Rose."

River and Glory didn't expect me until dinner time the following day, and I needed space between them and the secrets the photographs revealed. Not just the fact that Glory had a brother - never mentioned, hidden away in her heart forever, or maybe not important enough for her to think or talk about.

No, I struggled most of all with the image in Golden Gate Park. Glory's eighteenth birthday represented the last photograph my grandmother had of her daughter – taken eight months before I was born. I was haunted by the fact that my father stood outside the circle, more like an uninvited guest than the father of this child about to be born. The father of this innocent baby girl. The father of me.

I had imaginary conversations with both River and Glory as I drove in silence, avoiding all noise, not even the radio to distract me. Most stations were cluttered with nothing but annoying commercials, maybe twenty minutes of every hour devoted to the actual music. In some ways, I relished the idea of having almost two days to collect my thoughts in total silence, as well as time to prepare for the conversation I would have with my parents before I returned to school in September.

YOU WOULD HAVE THOUGHT I had been gone for twenty years. Glory heard my car tires crush the gravel on the winding driveway long before I reached the top. She waited for me on the porch, the front door wide open, a grin that could be seen from one hundred feet. I knew she couldn't wait for me to get home. In that moment, all of my anger, my pent-up emotion, and my well-rehearsed accusations vanished.

She had no idea what I had uncovered, what truths had been exposed, or that I was determined to find out more in the coming weeks. She was just happy I was home. River stepped into view and stood behind my mother, squinting at the setting sun, a can of beer in one hand as he waved an enthusiastic hello with the other. My mother was still beautiful, and my father still resembled the eighteen-year-old boy in the photograph. Slim, shoulder-length hair, and a trimmed mustache. The only thing missing was the beaded headband.

I chuckled to myself. *Thank God.*

The wet cloak of winter had made way for the dry spell of summer, and I could see the garden suffered from lack of water and care. The farm seemed absent of people. Although River and Glory never mentioned anything, they seemed like the only ones left, custodians of this massive plot of land meant to care for twenty families or more when this dream of their youth was born.

I surveyed the yard and the view beyond our home, communal houses separated by rows of overgrown bushes and shrubs. The tire swing dangled precariously from two thick lengths of rope, unraveling and worn from years of exposure to the elements. I saw no children. If there were any goats or chickens, I didn't hear or see them. I noticed one lazy dog that looked like a yellow lab and German shepherd mix. It lounged under the rocking chair in an attempt to stay cool. It didn't have the slightest interest in me, not bothering to look up when I climbed out of the car and ran to greet my parents. I thought Glory would burst into tears.

"I'm so glad you're home, Rose!" She threw her arms around me with strength and power I never knew she possessed.

River joined her, a bit more subdued, but obvious in his delight that I was home for the summer. He lived to make my mother happy. At that moment she was ecstatic, her emotional reunion with me, her girl, her daughter, all that she seemed to need.

I was happy to hear that Aunt Fern, Uncle Jacob, Destiny and her new husband, Ben, would be joining us for dinner. Letters between me and my best childhood friend were intermittent. I hadn't even told her about Andrew, although I couldn't wait to get her alone.

He promised not to say anything to his family until I called him and let him know I had told mine. Timing would be everything, and I ached to hear his comforting voice again. Had it really been just one week since our bittersweet good-bye?

"The farm seems quiet, didn't see much activity when I drove up."

That was as good a place to start as any. I managed to get River and Glory's attention after dropping my suitcase at the foot of the stairs, peeling off a jacket I didn't need, and plopping down on the couch. Not much had changed in the year since I had left, and yet everything felt different.

River joined me on the couch. "Thought it would be better to tell you in person, instead of on the phone or in a letter. You're not wrong. There have been some big changes."

"Such as?" I wondered if one of them was sick or dying. I could tell it was killing River, whatever he seemed intent on holding back. I waited for him to speak.

"Lots of new development around here, and builders have been swarming around the farm for the last five years."

I hadn't noticed. In high school, if anyone visited or suggested to my parents that they stood in the path of progress, thus preventing an eruption of housing projects and ribbon-cutting ceremonies, it was never mentioned.

"Most of us resisted, up until now. The money was too tempting for the majority of families. Everyone except our family, and your Uncle Jacob and Aunt Fern, took the offer and moved on. It's been just us for the last two months."

I hadn't expected this announcement, this explosion in lifestyle for my parents, money in the bank, probably enough income to last them the rest of their lives, and a lucrative offer they chose to refuse. My mind quickly rattled off all the reasons they should have taken the money and left with the other families, even though it was everything they'd fought so hard to resist for the past two decades. They both lacked an education and skills outside of the farm, with no apparent way to earn an income. To me, it sounded like an opportunity too good to pass up and a dream come true, yet staying put, when almost every other household seized their opportunity to flee, was their decision to make.

I eased deeper into the conversation with short questions, hoping for longer answers. For all my desire to escape for as long as I could remember, I knew my parents planned this existence for life. They disliked change. I could smell the aroma of warm biscuits wafting from the kitchen and my heart settled for a moment.

Glory kept her distance, preparing a Sunday dinner, even though it wasn't Sunday, to welcome me home for the few short months of summer. Nothing smelled better than our house when Glory made Sunday dinner.

I voiced my thoughts to River. "Why wouldn't you accept the money? It seems pretty lonesome up here now. Pretty soon, you'll be surrounded by homes, supermarkets, and public parks. I see it happening all over. I think they call it urban sprawl."

I felt knowledgeable and smart. I smiled when I recalled my conversations with Andrew. Mostly his lengthy dissertations about architecture, but in this instance, it helped.

"Well, I'm not finished here." River picked up a stack of forms, papers, and pamphlets and handed them to me. He reached for his reading glasses. This was a new development during my absence, as well. River didn't wear glasses. He cracked a smile. "Dime store readers." He balanced them on his nose, tilted back his head, and glanced at the glossy renderings before he handed them to me. "A Great Place to Raise a Family," the bold letters in a font size four times as big as the text shouted from the cover of the brochure.

In colors never seen in real life were children playing in well-manicured parks, families walking dogs down the tree-lined sidewalks, and older couples walking hand-in-hand beside a man-made stream amidst vast open spaces and meandering pathways. I had never seen grass that green, flowers that yellow, or a sky that blue. It was all meant to capture the imagination of potential buyers, who searched for something new that would define their ambitions and feed their purpose, much like my parents had discovered theirs. It didn't make much difference what the elusive fantasy was, we all have them, our own ideas of perfection, nirvana, peace. There was something for everyone in this slick portrayal of the new American community.

"Glory and I, Jacob and Fern, we didn't exactly turn them down, but we did find another way to negotiate with the investors and builders." A broad smile emerged on River's normally unemotional countenance. "It's not about the money to us, but about the freedom to do as we please, answer to no one, and live a peaceful, uncluttered life. No matter how much money we would receive, none of us wants to return to the city or urban sprawl as you call it, so we made a compromise."

I never knew River possessed the fight he apparently needed to deal with a powerful developer. Money talked, no matter where you lived. "And?" I encouraged as I continued to leaf through the marketing literature. I had to admit, it looked impressive.

"And, in exchange for selling our portion of the land, each

of us will retain one acre, along with a paved road and open space in between the development that can never be built on. They offered to construct one of their brand new homes for us, but neither one of us wanted that, so they will do improvements on the existing houses on the plumbing, electrical, siding, roof...things like that. We haven't hammered out the particulars yet or inspected the houses. Probably will need a lot of work – both of them."

"You seem pretty excited, River."

I looked around for Glory, but this was my father's moment. I heard her rustling in the kitchen. He was animated and lively, and I had never seen that side of him before. I was still absorbing the enormity of this information while he persisted.

"There's more."

He continued to pique my interest even as I marveled at his acceptance of the change that had come to his paradise.

"Good, bad?"

I had never before shared a conversation like this with River, and I felt privileged to listen to him open up and share his thoughts. He treated me like an adult instead of a child. I couldn't help but think there may have been times in his life that he had grown restless and bored with the easy-going lifestyle that had once seemed like a good idea. Maybe he regretted the fact he never attended college, or that he wouldn't ever find a job in the outside world even if he had wanted to. Maybe he had settled, and after a time accepted that this was the place he would know until he took his last breath. This opportunity had ignited a spark in him, and I felt genuine enthusiasm in our conversation.

"Don't know yet. Let's just say it's different. Builder says he wants to turn the roadside stand into a permanent structure, a small market that keeps the original ambiance and mood of the temporary setup we've managed for years. Even wants to erect a billboard at the highway exit to entice drivers to pull over for a farm-fresh bag of apples or pint of just-picked strawberries." River shook his head, but the smile never left his face. "They want to call it 'Commune Fresh Market.' A line underneath would say, 'We don't sell anything unless it's in season.' How absurd is that?" He looked resigned, but not unhappy as he turned to me for my opinion.

My opinion...I could tell it mattered to him.

I had learned a thing or two while I was away and recollected my class in Marketing 101. "Sounds pretty cheesy, but they have departments made up of well-educated public relations and marketing types with dozens of years of combined experience under their belts. I'm sure they know what they're doing to create the mental image of the new combined with the old. Almost like they're preserving a piece of the history so they can't be blamed for blemishing the original concept or serenity of the environment. It's a common marketing strategy, and as glossy as their brochures."

I delighted in my ability to converse on this level with my father. "You and Uncle Jacob, Glory and Aunt Fern - what will you do?" I couldn't imagine them sitting around in rocking chairs all day doing nothing.

"Already settled. We'll manage two additional acres they set aside for growing fruits and vegetables year-round, and we'll also run the store. They've already hired Ben, Destiny's husband. It'll be good to have young muscles to help out with the heavy lifting. Money is good...worked that out, too. Let those developers have their dream, as long as they don't take ours."

River looked pleased, satisfied that he had been able to maintain a lifestyle of self-sufficiency while adjusting to the changes that had been thrust upon him. He reached out his hand for mine, a gesture foreign to me.

"My Rose," he said in an almost inaudible tone, "I've never told you how proud I am of you. Not just now. I always have been. I've stood by in awe as I watched you grow, mature, work hard to follow your heart, and then harness that independent spirit you were born with."

I reveled in his sentiment even though I felt uncomfortable. I was speechless. I looked down at our two hands touching. I didn't remember ever holding his hand, not even as a child. I'd been left largely on my own to explore with Destiny and the other children. If we ever went into town, it was with our mothers, who managed to keep a firm grasp on us as we navigated street lights, department stores, and throngs of strangers. Never with River, never with Uncle Jacob. They worked all day, ate supper, went to bed early and rose before sunrise.

This was a moment in time that would never leave me. Even though I could feel the tears welling in my eyes, I managed to stammer, "Thanks, River."

My normal, articulate self was at a loss for words, especially when he let go of my hand and drew me close for a big hug. "I'm honored to be your father. Thank you for being you, Rose, and for staying true to yourself."

He gently released me. My mind raced. Where was all this coming from, and why now? A bundle of emotions enveloped me, my plans to approach River and Glory about my parentage before I returned to school now questionable and put on hold.

I was happy, I really was, but surprised by this side of

River I had never seen before. Maybe if he had been the kind of father who read me stories, took me fishing, or spent an afternoon playing ball, I would never have engaged in this quest for answers that I had saddled myself with for almost a decade. I abruptly changed the subject. I must have sounded rude to River, even though it wasn't my intention.

"I have some news to share with all of you at dinner, too." Before he had the chance to question me, I jumped up and headed towards the kitchen. "I'm going to help Glory...smells so good."

I decided not to say anything about the photograph. Not tonight. I would think of a way to broach the subject some other time. For now, it was all about family.

THE DINNER TABLE WAS FILLED with small talk. Destiny glowed. She sat across from me, her head resting on her husband's shoulder, both of them sneaking the occasional pat on her stomach like no one else was around.

"How many months, Destiny?" I secretly wondered how she could look so beautiful, even more than usual. Would I be as radiant when it was my turn? Would I even have a turn?

"Almost seven months." She gave Ben a look of adoration as she patted her soon-to-be baby again. "I've never been happier, Rose."

"I can tell. Seems like we've both missed so much with each other's lives. You never think it's going to make any difference when friends move away, you always hope to have enough time to catch up with phone calls and letters, but before you know it, major changes have occurred."

I shook my head. I was trying to take in the news all at

once from my parents and my best friend and I couldn't believe I almost ruined everything with my heartless thoughts. Then I remembered I had very big news too that I hadn't shared with them. I took a deep breath and took the plunge.

"Have any of you heard from Andrew lately?" I couldn't blurt out my news. I tested the waters to see if anyone had an inkling of what had happened between us at school.

Uncle Jacob offered, "Yeah, I did hear he's finishing his degree in San Francisco. You're at the same university, in case you didn't know." He started to take a bite of the golden, warm, biscuit, dripping with butter and honey, but held it back from his mouth as if to add the postscript before he devoured the familiar flavor that never disappointed the taste buds. "My brother did mention a few months ago that he had a girlfriend and he had never seen him so happy....but that's all I know."

Destiny looked crestfallen for me. She knew my crush on her cousin had lasted years, destroyed any chance of a dating life in high school, and she felt I had thrown away four perfectly good years pining for someone I could never have. I didn't let her struggle with her thoughts too long. I cast a demure smile in her direction. One only she could see. I noticed her eyebrows arch as she instantly read my thoughts and understood without words.

"Have you ever run into him on campus?" she asked coyly, playing with the situation, and enjoying every second of our charade.

"Yes, I have...I did...at a bonfire last February..." I had to let it loose. I felt too elated to hold this news in much longer, especially after hearing Uncle Jacob say that Andrew had never been happier. "We've been inseparable ever since. I'm the girlfriend...I'm the girlfriend!"

I realized how childish I sounded, like I might have if Andrew had asked me out when I was in high school. I knew this was what the color of love looked like. I felt Destiny's elation of impending motherhood and finding her perfect mate, my parent's devotion to one another for over twenty years, and the peace that comes with an indisputable sense of unconditional love.

CHAPTER 16

Destiny knocked first, then let herself in and made her way to the old recliner. I missed the activity and background noise of the other families and children who would never return. I also thought about the fact that this simple existence would soon be shattered by paved roads, fast-food restaurants, and overcrowded malls.

I shuddered when I realized it would soon look like every other suburb that stretched beyond the city limits. As much as I loved the accelerated pace, I couldn't envision Glory and River living comfortably in the chaos. Or Destiny, for that matter. She had found contentment where I had not, and she never questioned her options. *Must be nice to be so sure of yourself and your life.*

I looked up from my book. "Careful, Des, don't trip on the dog!" I catapulted out of my chair. The last thing we needed was for Destiny, who couldn't even see her own feet at this point, to take a fall and injure herself or the baby.

I tugged and pulled the old hound out of her path. He had managed to steal my heart and followed me everywhere I went. I could barely go to the bathroom without him tagging along, but at least he listened when I admonished him for trailing me when I needed privacy. Or maybe it was the Milk Bones I kept in the deep pocket of my shorts. Whatever it was, he was semi-obedient, and I knew I would miss him when it came time to return to school.

"How do you manage to look so beautiful, Destiny? Not only are you eight months pregnant, it's hot, sticky, humid...I'm a mess, and you're radiant."

We greeted each other in the middle of the living room and managed a warm embrace around her expanding belly. I patted it and understood the allure of resting your hand on a growing human being, even if it was hidden from view. Destiny wasn't shy about sharing her soon to be born child with the rest of the family.

I fetched each of us a tall glass of decaf iced tea. I retrieved the peanut butter and jelly sandwiches I had prepared, wrapped in waxed paper and packed in two brown lunch sacks. Each bore our names written in bold, red crayon. I intended for us to picnic by the stream, as much for the sake of nostalgia as a way to beat the heat, but I could see that my friend was far too pregnant to endure the half-mile walk to our childhood spot.

"Get comfortable. We're having an indoor picnic." I felt glad for this alone time with Destiny, my partner in crime since birth. We shared unique memories and we'd experienced an upbringing none of my school friends could fathom.

"Oh...peanut butter...the only thing I've craved for the last eight months. How did you know?" She peeled back the wax paper and didn't waste any time consuming the first half of the sandwich. "Do you have any pickles?"

I doubted she was serious and gave her a suspicious grin. "Really, Des? You're teasing, right? I thought that was an old wives tale."

"Could be, but yeah, you're right, pickles have not been high on my list...just testing you."

I could see she was enjoying herself, and so was I. Our spirited exchange of banter made me feel like we would always be best friends, no matter what the future held.

MY SUMMER BREAK REVEALED far less than I had hoped or planned. I wanted answers to my burning questions from River and Glory.

Did you share partners?

Did you sleep randomly with one another before and after you started the commune?

What's the real reason you haven't spoken to your mother in twenty years?

Most of all, I needed the answer to one particular question. "Who is my father?"

But with my new found wisdom, and Destiny radiant with her first venture into motherhood, I decided not to say a word on this trip. Maybe I would never know the truth.

I wished this gnawing in the pit of my stomach would go away.

CHAPTER 17

I saw Andrew from a distance as I pulled into the student parking lot. My heart skipped. We had spoken at least once a week during our separation. I shared the excitement that permeated our family with the birth of Destiny and Ben's baby boy one week before my departure, but nothing could replace seeing him in the flesh.

He was tan and solid from working all summer, dawn to dusk on his father's farm. It was hard to imagine him standing over a drafting board, locked inside a room with engineers, architects and secretaries. He didn't fit the part, stood out from his sun-deprived classmates who roamed the corridors of the School of Architecture and Design.

I checked myself in the rear-view mirror, and my hands shook as I applied one more round of lip gloss. I let Destiny talk me into a more daring hairstyle and I'd spent far too much money doing so. My hair had grown long and straight again.

I hadn't kept up with that first short cut. Too much work for my taste. Never high maintenance, I watched Cecily agonize over hot curlers, hair dryers, and flat irons every morning. She convinced me I wasn't suited to the two-hour ritual that looking perfect on a daily basis entailed. Most of the time I pulled my hair away from my face in a non-glorious ponytail or braid, and that's how Andrew was used to seeing me. I didn't recognize myself as I glanced at my reflection one last time.

"Your hair is so gorgeous," Destiny had gushed. "But it needs a trim...it needs a style." She would know. She studied every beauty magazine for make-up tricks, fashion, and hairstyles. "Here." She shoved the cover of the latest Glamour magazine in my face as we sat on the porch, searching for shade, one week before her due date. It was like old times, except we both knew our worlds would be turning corners and the dreams we once shared were here. With her outstretched hand, barely able to move, she passed the magazine to me and pointed to the cover.

"Now that's a hairstyle that would look great on you. It's called The Rachel. I think it's named after some actress on a TV show." I was aware of the TV sitcom. There were no televisions in the commune. I felt disconnected from my best friend's world as she devoured the images before her.

She flipped through the magazine as we huddled close together, heads down, like when we were little, analyzing pictures that sprung to life on the pages before us. With every turn, a new air-brushed model sported the same bouncy, square-styled cut. Bangs covered their beautiful faces, large expressive doe eyes peered out from frosted tendrils, and their mouths parted with just the right amount of girl-next-door sex appeal.

"You live in a city, not on a farm. Time for a new look, my dear friend, Rose. Especially if you want to turn Andrew's head the next time you see him." She pointed emphatically to the cover photo again. I couldn't say no.

Andrew spied my car and started walking toward me. The

closer he got, the more nervous I became. I started to dig through my glovebox for a rubber band, a twisty, a ribbon, anything. I regretted that I had listened to Destiny, and I felt sure he would be disappointed instead of pleased at what I had done to my hair. He picked up his pace and broke into a run.

I had no choice but to get out of the car and greet him, wrap my arms around him, and feel the warmth of his body next to mine once again. The ache in my heart started to disappear as I realized we were close enough to touch, and I detected a look of approval as he scooped me up and into his arms.

He nuzzled my neck and whispered, "I don't know what you did to yourself over the summer, Rose. You were already gorgeous, but now you're breathtaking."

I was thinking the same about him, and any misgivings I had about our homecoming melted into the background.

ANDREW STAYED ON CAMPUS one more year to finish his degree. I never warmed to the idea of pushing my fantasy on him...my daydream to share an apartment as boyfriend and girlfriend, or husband and wife for that matter. For all his good looks, confidence, and charm, he was old-fashioned and didn't believe in living together.

My grandmother allowed me to spend my room and board allowance on a small apartment close to campus, which gave Andrew and me more privacy than my dorm room. I yearned to talk about our future, but I didn't want to push him away. I knew I was far more anxious than him to feel the security of a commitment. Not that we were seeing other people, but the lack of a ring on my finger or the spoken desire to find a place large enough for the two of us made me feel apprehensive about our entire relationship.

Our conversation took an uneven path when we discussed the validity of communal living. I reminded him of my upbringing. "What about our parents?" I off-handedly posed the question to him.

"You mean your parents, don't you, Rose?"

We were lounging in our favorite coffee shop on Fisherman's Wharf. The air smelled fishy that Saturday morning. Even with the dense fog and bone-chilling dampness, Andrew wanted to get as far away as he could from campus.

We were both itching to put our educations behind us and start our adult lives and our careers. We viewed the incoming freshmen as children.

"I still don't know much about your folks, Andrew. All I know about mine is that your Uncle Jacob and Aunt Fern, along with Glory and River, left home together at eighteen. My mother was pregnant with me, and Aunt Fern was pregnant with Destiny...at the same time."

I started to think of a way to dodge this conversation I'd started and now regretted when I noticed the disapproving expression wash across Andrew's face.

"Didn't know that. Did you always know? Not my style or intent to get a girl pregnant before marriage. My parents did it the old fashioned way with a big church wedding, a honeymoon, and a respectable amount of time between the wedding and my birth. A long time, actually...almost five years."

His tone sounded accusatory and opinionated. I began to doubt his overall flexibility. Still, I asked, "Why did they wait so long to start a family?"

The coffee shop started to fill with tourists, noisy children and irritated parents doing their best to settle their children. The hot chocolate machine was on overload as parents coaxed the little ones to the farthest corner seats. As soon as one family would vacate, another would fill the empty chairs.

The powerful aroma of coffee and chocolate, donuts and freshly baked cookies thankfully overtook the stench of the outside air, but the noise level remained at a din, and meaningful discussion proved difficult. It could have been the topic. I chose to believe it was the commotion that surrounded us.

"I never asked. I don't pry, like you. Did they tell you?" he pressed.

"No. I saw a picture in Grandmother's photo album. It was Glory's eighteenth birthday, and it was taken eight months before I was born. I did the math. It was the last picture in the album, so I assumed it was when she and the others left to start the commune. There are a lot of gaps."

"Such as?"

"I thought you weren't the curious type." I cast a playful look in his direction, looking for a clue as to whether he was really interested or making conversation. His expression didn't change.

"Well, you started it. What do you think caused your parents to up and leave the city so abruptly?"

Our conversation was heading in a direction I had not intended. I drew a deep breath and blurted, "In the picture, your Uncle Jacob was standing next to Glory. River was in the background."

"So, what does that prove?" Andrew was oblivious to the impact of the image I was trying to create. "Weren't they all good friends?"

I danced around the obvious. "Yes, but I was wondering

why my father, River, stood in the background, while my pregnant mother was standing next to your Uncle Jacob. It seemed off somehow."

Andrew looked more exasperated than intrigued. "If you are insinuating that my Uncle Jacob is your father and River is not, that's absurd." He took a big gulp of coffee and a bite of bear claw too big to swallow, as if trying to eat the words being forced out of his mouth. He leaned in and whispered, "Jacob is not your father, my love. The ramifications of that thought running around in your pretty little head would be that you and I are cousins and I don't believe that for a moment."

Of course, I had mentally done the lineage many times, but I pushed it into the farthest corner of my brain. If Andrew and I WERE cousins, it would prove disastrous to our relationship. I regretted mentioning anything and quickly changed the subject. "You're right. I'm being silly."

"Yes, you are. We have our whole lives ahead of us, and I want you in mine as long as you will have me. Quit making up stories in your head and think about how wonderful we are together, here, right now."

I grabbed his hand, warm even though there was a chill in the air, and entwined my fingers in his. It was a rare moment of peace in my mind. He firmly clasped my hand in response. "I want you to meet my parents, Rose. I've been gushing about you for a year, and it's past time. How does next weekend sound?"

CHAPTER 18

It happened much sooner than I anticipated. My life took on a dreamlike quality from the moment Andrew asked me to marry him. I felt liberated instead of restrained, having created an identity separate from my parents and moved away from an upbringing that never suited me.

Andrew and I didn't talk about my suspicion that River might not be my father. At our wedding, the old friends and family mingled as though they had never been apart. Grandmother, hesitant at first, accepted the invitation from Glory and River to join us, and I escorted her to the farm a few days before the wedding. I never did find out what kept her and Glory up all night in the kitchen, cooing over a bowl of ice cream, or on the front porch, watching the town lights sparkle in the distance. My heart warmed at the thought of them enjoying each other's company, and I remained an onlooker.

The commune had started to transform from the remote, open land I knew as a child, and the first home communities sprang up in the distance. The apple orchard closest to the highway was now a busy intersection with a gas station on one corner, a Safeway supermarket on another, and a block of small businesses to serve the new homeowners. The

Commune Fresh Market had been built, as promised. Though it looked out of place at first glance, it seemed to be the sustenance that fed the perception of a natural way of living, even though one could almost touch the sides of your neighbor's home, and the two-story cookie-cutter palaces blocked the sky.

The change was profound, but no one seemed to mind, especially my mother. I suspected that security was something she thought about the older she got, even if it was not even a glimmer of a notion in her youth. As promised, River and Glory's, Uncle Jacob's and Aunt Fern's homes were transformed with all the modern conveniences. Their plot of land was surrounded by ten-foot-tall arborvitaes that preserved their privacy and blocked prying eyes from the outside a few hundred yards down the hill.

Destiny, Ben, and their one-year-old son, Seth, stayed put on the commune. They enjoyed living in the basement apartment her parents had coerced the builder to complete well after negotiations had been finalized. It was something of a struggle to convince them, but in the end, the remaining members of the commune were rewarded with enough land to support their families and sufficient cash in the bank to cover any expenses that might occur during their lifetimes.

My friend was content, having married a man who seemed as at home with the living arrangement and lifestyle as she was. He, River, and Uncle Jacob worked side-by-side at the produce market. I was glad he was there to help. My father and uncle weren't getting any younger.

Even though it had been my choice to leave, I was now the separate, independent daughter, off to conquer the world and show everyone how fabulous a life of material wealth could be. Andrew and I would be living in the city, in a small rented apartment, as soon as we returned from our honeymoon. I always wished we had given living together a try before the wedding, but my old-fashioned, handsome guy wouldn't hear of it.

"And don't you look beautiful, Rose!" my mother gushed as Destiny adjusted the veil. I took one last look in the mirror...from the front...side...behind, my neck twisting around like a parrot as I struggled to see my backside and what the guests might view as I walked down the aisle to my groom.

I didn't feel nervous. I simply hoped I could take Andrew's breath away when he saw me take the first step down the aisle. Every hair was in place, Destiny helped me apply just the right amount of makeup, the weather blended a fall breeze with summer sunshine, and even I had to admit that I glowed.

I walked carefully towards Glory so as not to disturb my flawless appearance. Tears welled in her eyes. I pondered, but just for a second, if they were tears of joy, or if she was thinking back on all the years that had come before this day.

I wondered if she was holding onto something she would never reveal. If one day I found the courage to approach her with all of my questions, which burned inside me since I was young enough to understand how babies were made, how would she respond? It was a flicker of a thought, banished when I saw my mother, in all her sweetness, reach out to embrace me. I returned her warm gesture as I almost wept.

IT HAD BEEN YEARS SINCE I had been to a wedding on the grounds of the commune. Andrew and I had never attended one together. We didn't want anything fancy, but our mothers, and grandmother as well, insisted on a small degree of tradition.

My groom wore a tuxedo with a royal blue cummerbund and a boutonniere made of a single white rose. Just when I thought he couldn't get more handsome than he already was, my heart raced and my stomach fluttered when I spied him standing on the altar with the minister, his father standing for him as his best man.

This is my future. This is where I always wanted to be. This is my beginning and my end. Oh, Andrew, I hope you know you still make my heart race with anticipation every time I look at you. This feeling is one I will carry with me for a lifetime.

I slowly placed one foot in front of the other. I had seen enough movies to know that keeping everyone in suspense and making as grand an entrance as possible was the entitlement of the bride - my moment - and the one and only time I would take this walk.

I savored being the center of attention for the first time in my life. I wanted everyone to look at me and be awed by my radiance as a bride. Most of all, I wanted Andrew to feel the same way about me as I did about him.

Out of the corner of my eye I saw a gesture so subtle, I doubt anyone saw it but me. Next to an empty seat that River would fill once he handed me off to Andrew was my mother, dressed for the occasion in a new, floor length, chiffon dress with matching jacket. It draped and hugged in all the right places, the robin's egg blue of the fabric one shade lighter than her eyes.

We had shopped together for the first time in a real department store, and now we both wore something with a manufacturer's price tag that had never touched the skin of another human being. I'm sure Glory did this for me. She would have been happy with another trip to the formal section of a thrift store and would have looked every bit as stunning, but she agreed, it was my 'something new'.

Beside her, Uncle Jacob, Aunt Fern, my grandmother, Destiny, Ben, and their well-behaved toddler filled the remainder of the front row. They stood, all eyes on me. I cast a glance in their direction and noticed what I thought was more than an off-hand signal. Uncle Jacob leaned in towards my mother and whispered something imperceptible. To anyone else, an unimportant and fleeting few words.

I turned my eyes back to Andrew as swiftly as I had cast them aside, forcing myself to quell my uncertainty. I told myself that this day would not be ruined by real or imagined pasts and surrendered my thoughts to the present as I inched closer to the love of my life. I focused solely on my handsome groom, relaxed and in control as he waited for me.

My father gently kissed my cheek and nodded as Andrew took my hand and enfolded it into the familiar warmth of his. I prepared to give my pledge, my promise of a lifetime, to love, honor and obey forever. When we made the return trip down the aisle as husband and wife, Andrew wrapped his arm around my waist and pulled me close, sneaking little kisses until we passed the last row, an affirmation of his love for me and my realization that I had just become the luckiest girl in the world.

CHAPTER 19

Her sweet cry awakened both of us in the middle of the night. Andrew was always the first one to rush to her aid. I moved a bit more slowly, hampered by an emergency C-Section two weeks before Caroline was due.

She wasn't planned, but with all the lovemaking the first year after we were married, it was bound to happen. Ending the pregnancy was never an option, but that left us precious little time to find larger accommodations for the three of us – the studio apartment we hastily rented in the Haight Ashbury District of the city was no place to raise a child.

I had received my degree in Interior Design the spring before our wedding, but Andrew still had two more years to go in order to complete his Masters in Architectural Engineering. I held down a part-time job in a trend-setting boutique during most of my pregnancy, until complications forced me to stay in bed for the final two months.

Andrew worked five nights a week, stocking warehouse shelves, and he brought in barely enough for the two of us to survive. We felt the choice to live frugally in the beginning was a wise one, since neither one of us wanted the help of our parents, even though all of them had offered.

A two-bedroom apartment, twenty miles outside the city, was the trade-off for larger quarters. We were fortunate to find an available end unit. The windows that stretched from the floor to the ceiling allowed enough light into the rooms to create the illusion of spaciousness, and the fresh breeze was a welcome bonus to replace the stale and motionless air. Still, I sometimes thought of how Glory and River might perceive these close living conditions, a total contrast to their idea of freedom and their ability to roam at will.

I wondered if I was cheating my child by serving up these cramped conditions to her, necessitating a planned outing just to put her toes in a slow moving stream or to dig in the dirt with a bucket and shovel. My longing to leave the commune never wavered, but there were times when I understood my parent's perspective in casting off the trappings of a life centered on material things.

"Thank you, Andrew."

My outstretched arms welcomed our little miracle. Andrew placed her gently in the crook of my elbow, always left side first. For some reason, Caroline preferred that breast to the other when her inner clock told her it was time to nurse. She was new to the world, barely two weeks old, but already the three of us found a rhythm that drew us together as a family.

Effortless, natural, and tired beyond anything we had ever imagined, Andrew and I worked together like a fine-tuned performance engine. His mother had come and gone, having spent the first few days with us after Caroline and I came home from the hospital. Glory, River, Aunt Fern, and Uncle Jacob offered to help, but Andrew and I preferred the company of no one until I had more strength to spend time with relatives.

Andrew was all the comfort I needed, and I found that, even though I still felt weak, and it took me three times as long to complete a task, it was his presence I wanted, not a crowded apartment with doting grandparents and constant interruptions, all of it given in the name of help. Grandmother was too ill to travel the short distance from the city to our new home.

Worry was a new emotion for me, and the minute Caroline was born, coupled with the failing health of my grandmother, I wrapped it around my body like a cloak and learned it would be with me for the rest of my days. Motherhood plants seeds of doubt, dread, and joy all at the same time.

During the day, when Andrew was away, I spent Caroline's every waking moment with her in my arms, gazing down at the perfect person her father and I created. When she slept, I couldn't bear to put her in her crib so I often spent whole afternoons with barely six inches between us. My heart felt at peace, nothing mattered except the unconditional love that had come with being a first-time mother and the realization that we were a family.

As soon as Andrew walked through the door, whether it was for the evening or a break in between classes and work, we joined forces again to dote and revel in this perfect human being that was a part of each of us.

"You look exhausted, my love. Why don't you put the baby in the crib to sleep and get a little yourself?"

My husband pried her from my arms. I tired easily, and I didn't reject his offer to help.

"No, you look exhausted." I studied his face, handsome and open, but weary. I supposed we both needed a good night's sleep to combat our fatigue.

With Caroline safe and sound in her crib, Andrew drew a deep breath and plopped down beside me. "Ten minutes, that's all I need, ten minutes." Without opening his eyes, he pulled off his t-shirt, rolled over on his stomach and tugged at my hand, strategically placing it on his shoulder. "Could you rub my back, Rose? I miss your touch. I love our baby girl, but I want to curl up with you alone...please?"

He sounded plaintive and juvenile, but I knew what he meant. I obliged by caressing his bare skin, taut and muscular, until he fell asleep.

I THOUGHT IT WAS CAROLINE when I was suddenly jolted from my sleep, but it was the phone, randomly tossed to one side and off the cradle for at least an hour. It was a wonder there was any battery life left.

Andrew was out like a light and my momentary thought of jostling him and asking for help vanished when I saw how peaceful and content he looked. Nothing could wake him at this moment anyway, I decided, and thought another twenty minutes would be my gift to him before I would need to awaken him for his night job.

I crawled out without disturbing him, but felt cheated by the interruption. "Hello?" I'm sure the person on the other end could tell I was not happy. It was my mother.

"Rose? I know you and Andrew are worn out, and I wouldn't bother you if it wasn't something important."

Spit it out...just say it.

"Hi, Glory. No, Andrew and I were just taking a little nap. Neither of us have gotten much sleep lately. Is everything okay?

"No, not really."

My heart started to race. Bad news always began with a phone call and ended with a monumental moment of grief.

"It's your grandmother."

Tears started to well in my eyes before my mother could even tell me what was wrong. I wanted to ask, but decided to let her finish. It would get revealed soon enough.

"She's gravely ill, Rose, in San Francisco General... in the city. I've spoken to the doctors and they believe she will not be going home."

She's going to die. No one ever wants to say that word.

I tried not to sound panicky. "Why didn't I get a call? How long has she been in the hospital?"

"Apparently, I was listed as her emergency contact number. For years, I guess. Rose, I can't get into this conversation right now. River and I are making plans to get down there as quickly as possible, but I thought you might like to know...in case you want to go see her."

Glory's voice sounded doubtful, but I was mentally brushing my teeth, throwing on some clean clothes, and grabbing Caroline from her sleeping state and waking Andrew from his. In seconds, I felt energized and knew what needed to be done.

"Don't worry, Glory. It's all right. Andrew and I will get there. He'll have to call in sick to work. I'll see you and River soon. Call me...or find me at the hospital."

"Of course. We should be there by tomorrow." I thought I heard a faint comment from Glory before she hung up. It sounded like, "I hope we're not too late."

CHAPTER 20

Glory and I faced the enormous task of sorting through Grandmother's belongings. Caroline slept peacefully in her Moses basket, a gift from my parents. Even though it had been made popular with my mother's generation, I had to admit it was convenient and practical and would last until Caroline was at least three months old. I was happy it was portable and easy to lug around.

I saw too many mothers at the playground, exerting all of their physical strength on over-priced strollers that needed to be unlocked and unfastened; latches that needed to be released, screws that needed to be turned clockwise – or was it counter-clockwise - and ties that needed to be secured with the precision of a seasoned deckhand. I didn't consider it necessary to perform this ritual for the sole purpose of creating a comfortable place for a baby to nap for thirty minutes, only to collapse in reverse the cumbersome contraption that took extraordinary strength to heave in the back of a car.

"I wish I had saved yours, Rose." Glory moved gently towards Caroline, a dreamlike vision compared to the one that surrounded us in her mother's decaying and crumbling home. She caressed the soft cheek of her new granddaughter, then slowly withdrew her touch so as not to waken her.

"It would have meant so much more, but it was used to begin with and I couldn't bear to think of our precious grandchild in a battered, second-hand basket, held together by extra twine and stitching."

I couldn't get mad at Glory for her reasoning, even though I muttered, "Good enough for your daughter, but not your granddaughter?"

"You know what I mean, Rose. And those were different times. I've changed, River's changed, you've changed. It happens. Life is lived in cycles. Just because you cling to one idea as a youngster, doesn't mean you always have to think and feel the same way your entire existence. Every decade you live adds a new dimension and perspective. I had my turn being a mother and raising a child. You had your turn being a child. Now, you get to take your turn as a mother. Circle of life."

"You make it sound so simple."

"It is. Life isn't hard. People make it that way."

I pondered her words while simultaneously taking in the disorderly rooms before us. I felt sad for Glory that she'd been unable to talk to her mother, touch her hand, whisper good-bye, one last time.

I was the only one in her hospital room. I thought of Grandmother's obituary as we clung together during her last few moments of life. I created a paragraph in my head, then another, and another. Every one I had ever read said something like, "She died peacefully surrounded by family."

Is one person being surrounded by? Did this wonderful woman live so many years to have just one person by her bedside in her final moments? Would her obituary read, "Surrounded by one? Surrounded by her family?"

I tried to shake the thought, concentrating instead on the labored breathing that belied the serene expression on her face. I wanted to ask her what else she knew...about Glory, Uncle Jacob and River. I chided myself for being so self-serving. I loved my grandmother, I didn't want her to leave, but my heart continued to burn for answers. Sadly, I would not get them from her.

Memories seeped from every corner of the house, and it seemed like even those that were invisible could be touched. The old Victorian had fallen into a sad state of disrepair, which before now, I hadn't noticed. Grandmother never complained. She must have been comfortable being rooted in her past and our busy lives rarely intersected after Andrew and I married.

As my eyes darted upwards to the ceiling, I noticed the aged and peeling wallpaper, crown molding beginning to disintegrate, and light fixtures flickering from useless bulbs or electrical problems. I couldn't shake my feeling of remorse. I detected a shift in mood from Glory, as well, as we toted Caroline from one lonesome room to another, a few cluttered with everyday belongings, but most empty and musty from lack of furnishings and use. It must have been hard for Grandmother to climb all those stairs, the older she got, and probably why most of her possessions appeared to be crammed into the bottom floor. Kitchen, living room, a small bedroom and bathroom. Everything she needed. The rest was wasted space.

"Is this house the same as you remembered, Glory?" She shook her head slowly and choked back tears.

We rummaged through paperwork, a stack of bills, antique dishes and silver, more than we could ever get through in one day. Caroline slept comfortably in her Moses basket.

Glory seemed intent on peering into one forgotten room after another, lingering at none until she stepped inside her childhood bedroom, the first door on the left at the top of the stairs. She gasped and pressed both hands to her mouth. Her muffled voice was just loud enough for me to hear her say, "She never changed a thing. This is the same room where I slept the night before River and I left."

"Didn't you go in here when you visited the last time? When your father died?"

Glory looked stunned and slowly backed out, closing the door before she turned to me. "No need. There was too much chaos that night and my mother put the three of us in the large guest room downstairs. Now I wonder if she did it on purpose."

"Would it have made a difference? I mean, would you have been sad or mad if you knew she never got rid of any of your things?"

"Who knows what I would have been. No sense in wondering what I might have or not have felt. It was just a shock to see the image frozen in time. Like a movie set."

We retreated from the top floor together, picked our way carefully down the stairs and into the living room. Caroline started to stir. I made small talk. "I bet there was a lot of life between these walls when you were little. It's a shame that you didn't have any brothers and sisters."

I never asked Glory about her older brother, who died before she was born, and I wondered if she would bring him up. As she saw me move closer to the photo on the side table, the one with the little boy on the porch waving an American Flag, she fell silent.

Grandmother had brought the photo, buried deep in her treasures from the past, back into full view the day after she shared with me the brief life of her little boy. I had passed it every time I went into the kitchen for a Dr. Pepper and ached for her memory of a child gone too soon. Maybe that's why she hadn't displayed the photo before then. Too painful.

I felt Glory beside me. "That was my older brother, Jonathan. He died from polio before I was born." In a timid-sounding voice, she added, "I don't think my father was ever the same. It was almost like he let my mother have me so she could fill the hole from the loss of this beloved child. I spent very little time with my father and hardly knew him, but Mother did her best. Did my mother tell you? I'm sure she did. Your inquisitive nature would have made it hard for you to see this photo and not ask questions." Glory sounded almost relieved with the thought that at least one family secret had been revealed.

"Yes, I knew. A long time ago. It made me sad that she lost her first born child, and a little angry that you never told me yourself. I never could figure out why everyone was so secretive about this, and many other things. I still don't know why you and River left San Francisco and traded this lifestyle for the commune. It couldn't have been just some hippie dream."

"What's to tell, Rose?"

I looked at my mother, eye-to-eye. This was my moment. "Is there something else you aren't telling me?"

"Such as?" Glory looked surprised, but in complete control. How could she know what I had been harboring inside my head for all these years? As quickly as I spit out the question, I mentally withdrew it, looking for a segue to another topic.

Not the time. Quit being so selfish. Her mother, your grandmother, just died. Set it aside for another time. There will always be another time.

"Oh, just curious, I guess. I always thought living under a roof of privilege was far better than choosing a life of poverty. I never got it, that's all." I wanted to move away from the conversation as quickly as possible and welcomed the interruption of my baby's gentle stirrings.

"Why don't you clear a place on the couch so you can change and nurse her." My mother seemed to heave a sigh of relief, as well. "I want to go through this stack of bills on the desk. See if I can find a will, a deed to the house, anything. It'll take months to sort out everything she left behind.

"FIND ANYTHING GOOD? Look at this poor old house."

River and Andrew barely made it past the threshold. River's shoulders sagged, his eyes darting from one corner of the room to the other. It was easy to tell he had not seen the place in years. "What happened?" It was a rhetorical question, his shock and dismay unmistakable. "Has it been that long?" He was talking to himself at this point, shocked at every turn as he wandered through the house.

Glory emerged with a stack of papers held together by a single rubber band. It looked ready to burst. "I found this on mother's desk. I was getting ready to open some of these envelopes. It looks like they might be important."

We all sat huddled together in the living room, Caroline the center of attention as she nursed contentedly. What a picture we must have made. My mother started to peel back the rubber band, which snapped at her touch. She picked one letter from the pile, the return address prominently displayed in the left-hand corner, America Commercial Bank. It held one page and at the top, centered, in bold letters, and underlined so as no one could confuse or misunderstand the message to follow, it read, "NOTICE OF DEFAULT." The rest of the letter was a blur. My mother lowered her head and released the tears that had been dormant and silenced until now.

When the last of grandmother's belongings had been packed, delivered, and stored in River's and Glory's home, everyone breathed a sigh of relief. The first shock had finally worn off. My mother stopped punishing herself for all the years she'd missed, and she set aside all of the questions that would never receive an answer.

I, on the other hand, continued to search for that perfect moment to approach with my own questions, even though I knew I might not get the answers I craved.

CHAPTER 21

Caroline seemed to become a toddler overnight. She had long outgrown nursing, middle of the night feedings, and her Moses basket. I tucked it away in a sterile, plastic, bag, sealed tightly for protection. I couldn't bear the thought of parting with it until Andrew and I made up our minds as to whether or not we wanted another child.

For now, our only daughter seemed like enough, but I had watched my friends become antsy for another as soon as their first started pre-school. Destiny already had two little boys and now awaited the birth of her third child. I never could figure out how effortlessly she grew her family, but she was a natural and she remained as gorgeous as ever. Her contentment obvious, she had found her perfect match in Ben.

It was like observing a better version of the original commune, complete with professional landscaping, updated plumbing, and modern conveniences.

Will I always be the outsider? I wondered. Will I always question everything I see and hear? You put yourself here. No one asked you to leave. This was your choice.

"IF YOU COULD LIVE ANYWHERE in the United States, where would that be?"

We had settled down in the meager and cramped back porch of our apartment we had long ago outgrown, and I placed the steaks, potatoes, and corn on the cob in front of Andrew. I never did learn how to cook with much expertise, and I would never become the wife that would have fresh biscuits and heavenly aromas drifting from the kitchen when my husband returned home after a long day at the office.

I lifted Caroline from the playpen and transferred her into her high chair, taking my seat between them. "What makes you ask?" It seemed like a delightful question, but random to say the least. I decided I would play Andrew's game.

"I've been thinking a lot about moving, not just because we're stepping over things and each other, but I really want to know. Do you miss the commune, now that it's a glimmer of its original concept? Or would you prefer the city? Maybe Southern California, or Arizona, or the East Coast?"

"So I would have a choice?"

I cut a piece of steak and speared it with my fork, twirled it a bit, studied it, like I was deep in thought at the prospect of so many options. I needed to think for a minute before responding. I paid no attention to the mess Caroline created on the floor, the corn I had cut off the cobb for her smeared all over the tray of her high chair, or the mashed potatoes in her hair. She wasn't complaining so neither did I.

"A choice of at least three now that I've been offered the position of Jr. Partner with the firm. It's expanding and they're opening offices in three new locations, plus keeping our flagship in the city."

Andrew looked sheepish and proud at the same time, and I could tell he was bursting to share his news with me. I almost knocked over the water pitcher when I jumped up from my chair to give him a congratulatory hug and a kiss that was more than a casual peck. I remembered Caroline was in the room.

Andrew, taken aback, grinned at me. "Wow, where did that come from? I haven't had one of those in a long time."

We were both a little flustered, used to stopping passion with a child present. A wink from Andrew assured me this night would be very special as soon as Caroline fell asleep.

I jerked my thoughts back to the present. "This is exciting, sweetie! I want to know...tell me...wait!" I thought out loud. "Southern California, Arizona, East Coast? Right?"

"You're so smart, my love, and gorgeous. A dangerous combination. So, where would it be? I have first choice over the other three guys who received a promotion at the same time."

"Do you care?" I proceeded cautiously. This was Andrew's moment, and I didn't want to spoil it for him.

"It will be our first real home, my pay raise was generous, and I want both of us to be happy. That's why I asked. I want this decision to be made by both of us, not just me. Think about it while we give our messy little girl a bath, and put her down for the night."

I stayed behind to do the dishes as Andrew scooped up Caroline and carried her to the bathroom almost before he finished his sentence. He looked back over his shoulder and winked again. My heart fluttered and that long-forgotten feeling of desire started to stir. It had been far too long since we had shared an intimate evening together, one of us too tired, a cranky baby in the midst, or a fading interest simply because we were becoming more and more uncomfortable in our crowded surroundings.

ANDREW RUSHED PAST ME with a dripping wet Caroline, giggling in her daddy's arms and not appearing at all tired. I kissed them both on the cheek as we intersected in the hallway.

"Don't worry, my love. I'll get her all bundled and dry in her warm footies and read her a story. She'll be out like a light in no time."

I felt like a high school girl babysitting her younger sibling while anticipating a make-out session on the couch. It was exciting and stressful at the same time. I dashed into the bathroom, quickly bagged the toys that had overtaken the tub, and drew the last of the hot water, filling it as high as it would comfortably go. I found an old bottle of bubble bath under the sink and poured it in its entirety under the gushing waterfall cascading from the spigot. Andrew appeared from out of nowhere, with a half-full bottle of Mateus wine that he found in the back of the refrigerator, two long stemmed wine glasses that we used for toasting at our wedding, and breathlessly announced, "She's asleep. I told you I could get her down in record time."

"You're hired," I teased as I started to peel off his sweatshirt and I felt the long-forgotten sensation of arousal. I didn't have to look. I could tell Andrew was feeling the exact same way.

Maybe it was because it had been so long since we had actually made love to one another that we went beyond the cursory sex that had become the norm. Maybe it was a burst of love so complete, I couldn't get enough of Andrew that night. Maybe it was a more mature woman, a mother, a wife, who responded to his touch and passionate overtures as though we had never done this act before.

Every movement from the soft, sensual kisses to the urgent, heart pounding moans of fulfillment, rippled through my body and brought an unfamiliar feeling of calm to my soul. There were no doubts, no questions, no concerns that night. I was completely and utterly at peace. I curled my body into Andrew's backside, still warm from our lovemaking and unhampered by clothing or covers. I murmured as we drifted off to sleep, "I want to stay here in the city. I don't want to leave."

He reached for my hand and entwined his fingers with mine. He drew me forward so that my head rested on his chest. "Me, too, my love. Me, too. Let's find a house big enough for four."

CHAPTER 22

That night created Nicole.

I remember finding comfort in Andrew's words, "a house big enough for four," but it wasn't meant to be a literal declaration. I wanted to wait another year or so before enlarging our family, especially now that we had decided he would stay at the city office and we would buy our first home. Definitely not good timing. In a way, I resented Andrew's good fortune, his ability to climb the ladder in his chosen field, while I was left at home to care for two small babies. It wasn't fair and it was not a happy pregnancy.

We looked for a house on the outskirts of the city, not far from our rental. We had become accustomed to the neighborhood, restoration was happening on every block and the window would soon close to the American dream of home ownership. Buying in town was quickly becoming the quest for the super-rich. Tech companies that didn't exist ten years earlier, were springing up all around us. The salaries were out of control, along with the escalating real estate values.

Andrew's firm found itself with more work than they could handle, and talk of further expansion ensued. He had certainly landed at the right spot, at the right time, as far as his career was concerned, and it was just the beginning. His keen eye for style and his work ethic and honesty made him the darling of the office with the elderly owners and partners. Eager to show them what he was capable of, he spent long hours away from me and Caroline, making the move even more difficult.

House-hunting during the first trimester of my pregnancy, and toting an eighteen-month old toddler to every Open House and scheduled viewing was grueling. With the higher pay came inflated home prices and lower inventory, making our search seem like an impossible dream. I wanted to settle on the first house we could afford and my grumbling quickly turned what should have been a magical experience into a nightmare.

Andrew did his best to play into my moods and whims. In the end, we found an older renovated home less than a ten minute drive from downtown. We became permanent residents of the Bay Area. Ironic, since my parents were raised and then fled a community that we embraced and where we would raise our children.

"Can't you be happy about this, Rose?"

I could see Andrew had lost patience with me, but he was away at work all day while I was home with one small child and another on the way. I hadn't made friends in our temporary housing situation in the cramped apartment that barely held the three of us - a place so small we couldn't invite family and friends to visit.

"I know this is a stressful time, but I just got a raise and we've just bought our first home. Can't you force yourself to smile every once in a while? We'll be moving out of here in a week."

I continued to fold the mountain of clothing that I had brought up from the laundry room, no easy feat while keeping a watchful eye on Caroline as she struggled to climb the stairs without assistance. Every step was unsteady and I held my breath as she teetered and swayed towards the landing.

"I did it, Mommy! I made it all the way up!"

The pride in her accomplishment was evident. Actually, with few words in her vocabulary, it was more like, "I did, Mommy...made up," but I understood what she meant. I balanced myself on the railing, the plastic laundry basket suspended on my outside hip, and joined her at the top. I was out of breath, but I managed to break a smile for my little girl. "You're so big, Caroline! I'm proud of you!"

She beamed.

Every day was an instant repeat of the one before. Up at five o'clock to shepherd Andrew off to work, a sip or two of coffee, a half cup if I was lucky before Caroline stirred in her crib and started to yell at the top of her lungs to pick her up. An impatient and loud toddler when she first wakened, she struggled to overcome the height of her crib, raised to the highest bar, which impeded her success but not her determination. I was generally in an irritable mood until I poked my head into her bedroom and we locked eyes.

"Is this my baby?" I would coo upon entering.

With outstretched arms, her response was always the same. "Up." "Out." "Now." followed by a charming smile that she had perfected from an early age. It was hard to remain in a bad mood for long.

By mid-morning I would have an energy spurt, enough to take Caroline to the community park two blocks from the apartment. She whined that she wanted to walk, leave the stroller at home, but I didn't trust myself in my rotund condition that I would be able to sprint after her if she loosened herself from my grip. I suppose it never occurred to her that if we hadn't brought the stroller, she would have had nothing to carry her home after an exhausted hour on the playground.

By noon, we were both worn out, even though housework beckoned while Caroline napped. The afternoon was swallowed by meal preparation, laundry, bill paying, cleaning, and by the time Andrew got home, Caroline was fed, bathed, read to, and ready for bed. The next morning, it started all over again.

"EVERYTHING IS SO EASY for you, Andrew. You leave at six o'clock in the morning and don't come home until seven o'clock at night. By then Caroline has been fed, bathed, ready for bed...fast asleep some nights."

I rolled my eyes, something I swore I would never do. "The movers are coming next week, and I haven't even sorted through what we're going to take and what will go to Goodwill." I halted my monologue and laughed out loud.

"What's so funny? You were just beginning to light into me. I thought I was going to have to dodge bullets the rest of the night."

"What's so funny..." I continued to fold a large bath sheet, methodically, matching corners, caressing the fine cotton and thick, luxurious fabric.

I had forgotten how I longed to shop for new things, anything with a price tag, feeling set apart by the fact that everything my parents owned was second-hand and every item of clothing on my back was originally meant for someone else. I was ashamed that I had ever felt angry at River and Glory, simply because they couldn't afford and wouldn't part with their hard earned money to pay full price.

With the final crease, I walked over to Andrew, now comfortable in the only chair in the apartment big enough to hold his tall, angular body. I inhaled once, swept away by the contrived scent of fabric softener meant to mimic sun-dried linens and reminiscent of the real aroma from my childhood. I placed the perfectly folded towel in his lap. "...is I'm giving stuff away to Goodwill instead of buying it."

My spirits momentarily lifted as I looked around the apartment, every corner crammed with items we needed and many we didn't. I had reached my goal, married Andrew, was about to bring a second child into the world, found a beautiful home in a neighborhood filled with parks, good schools, and other families like ours. I remembered the day Andrew and I parted for the summer to visit our families, and how I poked around neighborhoods like the one we'd just found to raise our family.

I arrived at my grandmother's flushed and animated, invigorated by the fantasy I had created. It was all I ever wanted, and my wishes had been granted. I processed my thoughts in rapid succession and bent over my husband to give him a kiss. Caroline jumped in between us to claim her father's lap, and I wondered why I felt so unhappy.

Your problem, Rose. You got everything you ever wanted, so be happy. Damn it, be happy.

I embraced them both, stood back, and smiled a smile that I hoped looked genuine and sincere in their eyes. "I'll make dinner."

WE MOVED FROM OUR tiny apartment to our spacious four-bedroom, three-bath home in the suburbs, met our neighbors, joined a gym, planned back yard barbeques, and welcomed Nicole, in that order. Maybe Andrew had been right. All I needed was to get out of our stuffy, confined quarters and breathe in the fresh air that came with wide streets, cul-de-sacs, and mature landscaping to feel grateful and content.

I never noticed the fruit trees in the back yard when we wrote the offer. Too busy complaining. I considered raising a bumper crop so I could can peaches, bake fresh apple pies, and try my hand at making plum jam, just like Glory used to, with very little luck passing the art down to her daughter.

I missed out on the joy of anticipation, the kind that bubbles up inside of you when something great is about to happen, something I should have been eager to experience with our new home purchase and a new baby on the way. But I more than made up for it when the dust finally settled, everything was unpacked, placed in all the right corners, and I established a routine for the four of us.

Andrew spent long hours at work, but weekends were a family affair. We had decided, at least in the beginning when the girls were little, to keep one extra bedroom for an office and the other for a guest room. I was eager to host our families for holiday dinners and large gatherings, something I'd never experienced. We never ventured out of the commune on holidays, except for the one I still vaguely remembered - that Christmas at Grandmother's house when my grandfather had been so ill. I wanted to create different memories for my daughters, not that mine were bad, but I didn't want their experiences to imitate my own.

Nicole was almost six months old and Caroline was an active, energetic 3-year-old with a full calendar of play dates. Every family's backyards hosted an array of playground equipment, and I slowly made friends through Caroline's popularity. Exchanging children for an afternoon was a welcome respite, and it gave me a couple hours to myself when Nicole went down for a nap. On the days when it was my turn to spell the neighborhood mothers, I brought out an arsenal of art projects, play-doh, and finger paints. I was the only mother brave enough to attempt this endeavor, and armed with yards of butcher paper that I spread out on the concrete patio, it soon became the favorite activity for anyone six years old and under.

Andrew's parents and sisters wasted no time in greeting the new granddaughter and second niece, understandable since they were only two hours away. River and Glory planned a leisurely trip from the Pacific Northwest, a day and a half drive even with the best of weather conditions. It was one of those trips that was too long for one day and too short for two, but I convinced them to spend our first Christmas in our new home with us. It wasn't the hard sell I anticipated. In fact, when I suggested they fly instead of drive, they jumped at the chance.

"One more thing, Glory," I said right before I hung up the phone. "Did you take any of Grandmother's photo albums from her house? Did you put any of them in storage?"

"You mean the set of leather ones with engraved dates and names?"

I pictured them in my mind. "Yeah, those are the ones. Do you still have them?"

"Every single one. I think there are about ten or twelve. I

don't think there will be enough room in the suitcase, and they're quite heavy. Any in particular?"

I could tell Glory was comfortable with whatever album I might suggest so I asked for two. "How about the one with your baby pictures and the last one, with your high school photos?"

I didn't want to come right out and say the one at your eighteenth birthday party. Maybe she would think that was a little strange. "I didn't get a chance to look at all of them after Grandmother passed. It was something I wanted to do."

I wasn't lying, it WAS something I had planned to do long ago. I had buried my suspicions the best I could, but unanswered questions continued to haunt me. Maybe Glory would have the answers.

CHAPTER 23

I couldn't deny it. When it came time to decorate the house for Christmas, I reveled in the prospect of designing the most fabulous living room, the most luscious tree, and the most self-indulgent ornaments we could afford. I had studied interior design for four years and never got the chance to use it. Our furnishings were adequate, but one day I would create a space that belonged on a coveted page of *House Beautiful*. For now it was populated with toys, leftover apartment furniture, and area rugs that didn't match.

Andrew never complained. For all the remarkable buildings he created, immersed in a six-day work week with some of the most talented architects in the city, he paid very little attention to the interior of his own home. As long as he was greeted with a smile and had a clutter-free place to stretch out, he was content. He urged me not to worry, reminding me that one day I could re-decorate to my heart's content.

"Don't come crying to me if the girls break any of these expensive treasures," were his only words of caution.

The weather held steady all Christmas week at sixty-five degrees, and we didn't experience the fog in our south part of town that hovered over the city throughout most of the year.

Regardless of the season, there were many days blanketed in a dense bank of impenetrable, moisture-filled, low-lying clouds that clung tenaciously to the skyline. No matter how romantic it appeared in photographs, or how many postcards were sold to tourists with the iconic Golden Gate Bridge enveloped in a billowy shroud, it made driving difficult and tempers short.

I didn't like the rain in the Pacific Northwest. Even though I chose to make the San Francisco area my home, fog was not necessarily a better option. Every street had a change in weather and we purposely chose ours based on the amount of sunshine it had on a daily average.

Flying was not something River and Glory did often, so I helped book a non-stop from SeaTac Airport in Seattle to San Francisco. On-time arrivals were almost guaranteed without layovers and with two hour flight times, incoming passengers felt energized as opposed to dragging when they disembarked.

River and Glory had only seen their first born granddaughter once, when grandmother died and Caroline was still an infant. I regularly mailed photos, the better ones framed. I shared every milestone. There's still nothing like face-to-face reactions and I had prepared Caroline the best I could about the impending visit from her grandparents. Many of her friends had two or more sets that lived close by, so she had some idea of who she would be greeting when we met them at the airport.

I was as excited for my little girl as I was for myself, and Andrew took full charge of Nicole while Caroline and I waited to greet them at the gate.

I realized this was a day of "firsts" for my little girl – first escalator ride, timid at first step, but eyes ablaze with excitement by the time we reached the top; first time getting to see an airplane land, upset with the roar of the engines, but mesmerized by the expansive glass walls with an endless view of the tarmac; a sea of travelers, children her age, dragging their own mini-suitcases behind them and child-sized backpacks full of toys strapped to their shoulders; and the mingling aroma of French fries and coffee that greeted us in the long hallways of the gated area. McDonald's beckoned within feet of my parent's gate.

"I want McDonald's!" Caroline shrieked, dragging me closer to the counter. "I want fresh fries!" Although her vocabulary was improving and quite large for a three-year-old, we considered her pronunciation of French fries too adorable to correct.

Certainly a classmate or friend would set her straight one of these days. When she finally settled in the seat closest to the window, her fresh fries went largely untouched and grew cold. She pressed her nose to the frigid glass, her strong toddler legs supporting her precarious balance on tiptoes. I suppressed a laugh when I saw her jump away from the window, the approaching 737 winding its way to its gate, the steward's announcement of the flight's arrival, and ground crew working like a well-oiled machine to connect the flight bridge to the now stationary giant bird. Caroline dashed into my arms, and I scooped her up in anticipation of greeting River and Glory once they disembarked.

CHRISTMAS EVE WAS MY FAVORITE night of the year, when the mundane surroundings took on a fairy-tale like quality and Christmas morning was hours away from bursting through the night. Caroline delighted in afternoon walks with River, her Papa, strolling through the neighborhoods, and lingering outside the house at dusk.

The moment the holiday lights went on, the street became a breathtaking vision of glowing icicles, and the rooftop Santa, who pulled eight reindeer with Rudolph in the lead, started to move with a believable rhythm of jolly old St. Nick in flight.

Caroline stood breathless, her eyes wide and her little hands clasped to her perfect rosebud mouth. "Oh, Papa!" she squealed. "Santa's on his way!"

A sudden recall of my childhood with River clenched my heart as I realized my recollections with him were far different. We were hardly ever alone, we never took walks, and I never sat on his lap to hear *The Night Before Christmas.* Try as I might, I couldn't summon one single memory of feeling like I was his treasure, his angel, his little girl.

I speculated that Glory might have felt the same about her own father, who practically abandoned her and grandmother the day she was born. If she did, she never talked about it, never criticized, never uttered a harsh word about either one of her parents. But it must have hurt...deep down, it had to hurt.

For our part, we recreated a snow-covered front lawn made of yards and yards of white, polyester, flame-retardant material, covered with white and silver glitter, and embedded multiple strings of white mini-lights in the cushiony boxwood hedge that encircled the front of the house. A mother, father, and two baby deer figurines stood under the large strawberry tree, twenty-five feet in height, with clusters of little pink, urn-shaped flowers that adorned it in late winter.

It was splendid in every season, with decorative edible fruit in the summer and lush foliage year round. It stood among many other identical trees on the block, and I gave a silent nod of approval to the developer of our community, who had the foresight thirty years earlier to choose evergreens with a lush canopy and a hearty survival rate.

A ring of vinca ivy remained visible at its base. Caroline hid bits of leftover toast and pancakes from breakfast, tucking them inside the vines to conceal them from view. She wanted to safeguard the morsels for the deer family and liked to think they had something to eat in the middle of the night.

We had to convince her they weren't going to starve and, sure enough, when she checked every morning to see if they had been eaten, every crumb was gone. We didn't have the heart to tell her it was birds, possums or squirrels raiding her secret stash, but we teased her without remorse when she was old enough to understand and no longer believed in Santa Claus.

I spent a fortune, far more than I should have. I thought about waiting until the day after Christmas to purchase the artificial wreath on sale, but it took my breath away when I spied it in the holiday lane of the local nursery. I knew I wanted a fresh tree and we were amply provided with dozens of choices at lots that cropped up the day after Thanksgiving, fresh trees arriving daily from Oregon. I had made up my mind I also wanted the fragrant aroma of fresh pine to greet visitors at our front door, but the majesty of the pre-lit and lushly decorated circle of simulated greenery dissolved my original choice.

I felt only a little guilty when I nonchalantly drew it from the box and asked Andrew to place it on the front door and center it on the wreath hanger that matched. He never asked, didn't question, merely switched the battery to the "on" position and joined me as we stepped off the porch and gazed together at our first of many traditional touches that would highlight our holidays as a family.

Andrew seemed pleased. "I'm glad your parents joined us for Christmas. I wasn't sure what to expect, but Caroline has taken to both of them, like they've always been around."

He led me back inside, where the lights were low, and the tree cast a glow that lighted the entire house. River, without asking, set out cookies and milk with Caroline for Santa, and Glory cradled Nicole. When she heard my voice, she knew it was time for dinner.

How could I doubt that River was my father? More than ever I wanted to purge that thought from my mind, but the nagging thought never let up. I viewed the touching scene before me, and I couldn't believe my thoughts had wandered to this incomprehensible question again.

IT WAS TOO PERFECT. Christmas Day was straight out of a storybook. Glory and I cooked all day, and I moved around effortlessly with Nicole, making good use of the baby carrier my mother had used for me when I was an infant. Her cherubic face pressed against my chest, and she didn't make a sound until dinner was served.

The Moses basket never made it out of the closet no matter how good my intentions at the time to use it with our second child. It would make a good doll bed when the girls got a little older.

The men watched football all day, ate too much, fell asleep during the third quarter, and roused just long enough in the fourth to devour two pieces of pie and a warm, fragrant piece of gingerbread with real whipped cream, dripping down the sides into a pool of liquid goodness. Caroline bounced from one lap to the next, spending no more than ten minutes with each person and five minutes with each toy. She grabbed cookies off a plate that sat in the middle of the coffee table, just the right height for a three year old. She delighted all of us by staying pristine in her taffeta, plaid dress with a large ribbon that tied at the waist and formed a glorious bow from the back. Her hair had begun to grow out, past the toddler curls. Long enough to now pull part of it away from her flawless face, the style showed off her expressive blue eyes. Just like Glory's. The day had been picture-perfect, and I was about to ruin it for everyone.

CHAPTER 24

I called Glory the day after they got home.

"Did you get a chance to look through the photo albums I brought? We were so busy, I forgot to ask. Why did you want those two books, anyway?"

I wasn't sure if Glory was suspicious of my intentions or not. Maybe she was just curious. How could she know what I'd been thinking for the last twenty years? Why would she ever consider I might not believe River was my father?

I had practiced this scene in my head for a dozen years. It was rotting my heart, and sucking the joy out of my life. I always knew it was my fault, not hers. Not River's. I wanted to be delicate, not put her on the defensive. I certainly wasn't prepared for where this conversation would travel.

I purposely found a quiet space in the living room, put Nicole down for a nap, and sent Caroline next door to play. I had already talked to Andrew on the phone during his lunch hour, and I didn't expect to receive a call-waiting beep during this exchange.

"I've been wondering something for a very long time, and I never had the courage to say anything. I don't want you to get mad."

"Why would I get mad?" Her tone bristled. I had already put my mother on the defensive. "Is this about something terrible you thought was perpetrated on you during your childhood? Are you so overwrought about being raised in a commune that you've carried it with you all these years? Is it about Goodwill and never having a new blouse, or a new pair of shoes, or a new lamp in the living room?"

If I hadn't been so well prepared to move forward, I would've laughed. I wondered if my mother might have carried some guilt of her own for raising me in such an unconventional fashion.

"No, Glory, I got past that a long time ago."

"Then, what?" Her voice sounded almost shrill. I had never know her to have anything other than an even pitch when speaking.

My tongue felt thick and my mouth went dry, but I couldn't stop myself. "It's about some photos I saw in Grandmother's album. It's about your older brother I never knew existed until she told me about him one day when we were looking at old photos, and it's also about an image I haven't been able to erase with you and Uncle Jacob at your eighteenth birthday party in Golden Gate Park. You and he were standing close together, while River stood in the background."

Glory snapped, "And what does that prove? Did my mother also tell you that your Uncle Jacob and I grew up together and had known each other since we were born? Did she tell you that her best friend was his mother, and he was over at our house every day after she died when we were in the tenth grade?"

My turn to be caught off-guard, but I continued to push. "No one ever told me about Uncle Jacob's mother and that she died when he was so young. But I do know her name was Rose!"

My voice started to rise. I had never been a screamer. I could picture Glory on the other end, twisting the phone cord and becoming more and more agitated as the conversation progressed. I thought she was close to hanging up on me.

"Again, what does that prove? Jacob's mother was a beautiful, loving woman, and Rose is a beautiful name. I thought it fit you perfectly, with your rosy cheeks and porcelain complexion, such a beautiful contrast to your dark eyes. It was an honor to be named for her."

I made an effort to bring us back on track, wanting to avoid the virtual collision we seemed headed towards. I visualized two mangled bodies after a sudden and violent crash, unsure if either driver would survive. But I pushed. "You never once mentioned your brother, didn't really talk much about anything when you were growing up. When I found out, I felt this nagging I had been fighting my entire childhood might hold some truth and there were more secrets yet to be told."

"I'm about to hang up, Rose, but please, what? What other secrets do you think your father and I have kept from you?"

I could tell she was about to cry, yet she was as insistent as I that everything come out in the open. If she would admit to any of my accusations remained to be seen. I braced myself for the big one. Both of us sounded ragged and afraid.

"I know what month you were born and I was acutely aware of what day your eighteenth birthday was. I also did the math, and I realized I was born eight months after that photo was taken. Uncle Jacob was right there...right there at your side, yet my father, River, was a fixture in the background.

Even Aunt Fern was standing close by." I heard Glory take a deep breath, as if preparing her rebuttal. "You have the deepest blue eyes I have ever seen, River the same. Uncle Jacob and I have the same brown eyes. According to my Biology teacher, it is impossible for two blue-eyed parents to have a brown-eyed child."

"Are you done?"

I was glad I didn't do this in person. I didn't want to see Glory's crestfallen face. I never intended to take this detour. I had hoped for an honest, open conversation between two grown women. Whether I struck a nerve because I had the impudence to open up this dialogue, or if her guilt had caught up to her after all these years and the secret she had kept was now exposed, was overshadowed by her response.

"This is a deep cut, Rose. You have managed to unravel a beautiful relationship that was just beginning to bloom with our grandchildren, you and Andrew. We were all about to enter a new phase in a beautiful life that none of us planned. You have smeared me and River with your vulgar thoughts and wicked imagination. I have nothing more to say. Please don't contact me or your father again. I don't think I could bear to look at you with the same admiration and love I have felt for you since the day you were born. Goodbye, Rose."

I tried to interject before she hung up, inaudible - no sound of the receiver settling into its cradle, no final swear word or reprimand, a deliberate absence of emotion. A faceless, dismal, and final farewell.

I instantly regretted that I had erased the possibility of a warm and affectionate future with my parents. Possibly forever. I wanted nothing more than to apologize, repair the irreparable, shout at the top of my lungs how sorry I was for cutting out her heart, and in the process, my own. I started to speak. Too late. She was already gone and I only had my imagination to let me know how she looked, felt, and ached once she severed the connection. My imagination that Destiny warned me about when we were kids, my over-reaction to a seed that I had planted to combat my boredom in the commune had now incapacitated me beyond repair.

I would never be able to fix this one. I took the risk and I failed miserably at making anything better for any of us. I ruined everything and only had myself to blame. How could I face Andrew? What would I say? For now, nothing.

Nicole started to stir from her nap. I dragged myself to her crib, leaned into her open and angelic face, and watched as she greeted her mother with an unquestioning and innocent expression of love.

CHAPTER 25

The months melted off the calendar like butter. Before I knew it, almost a year had passed. The holidays were upon us again, and my attempts to reach Glory proved unsuccessful at every turn. Letters of remorse and apology were sent back to me unopened, marked "return to sender."

Andrew was not aware and busy with work, so busy that he often stayed at the office well past dinner time and most weekends. It was easy for me to cover my tracks. I tried to make up for my grievous mistake by spending long hours with the girls, maintaining the house in proper order, and never complaining. I became passive and accepting, while I mourned the loss of my mother who was still alive.

I wondered if Glory had gone through the same thing after she'd left home, cutting her mother from her life when she had become pregnant with me. I recalled with sadness, that it took them decades to heal the wound that one of them had opened. I didn't know who was at fault. I grieved for the memories I shattered long before they could be made.

Nicole took her first steps about the same time Caroline started pre-school. She was precocious and social, gathering a network of friends from the neighborhood and the classroom.

She had taken charge of her life at four years old, and I was thrilled she fit in so easily with her playmates.

Andrew mentioned every once in a while that he hadn't heard me talk about my parents much since we put them on the plane back home. I became an expert at changing the subject. I didn't consider that he might have questions of his own as the gap between us widened.

We barely spoke and seldom made love. With my guilty obsession, I never considered he might be having an affair. As suspicious as my mind was about my past, I never questioned my present. I could not imagine Andrew with anyone else but me...even as I slowly pulled myself from his life.

Caroline prompted me to, "Call Papa. I want to say hello and tell him about my school."

I suggested she draw him a picture, which I included with the letters that always came back unopened.

Maybe Destiny would talk to me. We had lost touch as well, and I was certain my mother had told everyone about her terrible daughter and the ugly suggestion I had made to her. No doubt Uncle Jacob, Aunt Fern, Destiny and Ben harbored ill thoughts and told her never to speak to me again. I couldn't imagine being welcome in my parent's home ever again, even though I toyed with the idea of showing up one day on their doorstep to let the chips fall where they may.

My parents didn't own a computer, never thought much of email, but Destiny and Ben bought one for the sake of their children. They were savvy enough to know that even though they remained in the communal lifestyle with her parents and mine, the success of their sons and daughter would hinge on a modern education complete with cell phones, internet, and technical skills.

Thanks to the developers and a town that continued to

flourish around them, all these things were readily available to them. They frequently shopped at the strip malls and shops within driving distance, signed up for cable and internet, and enjoyed the best of both worlds.

Destiny...you always made everything look so simple.

I envied her more than ever.

I sat down at my computer as I had done every day. I hoped I could craft words far better than those I had used when I approached my mother. They were all wrong, accusatory, and she had reacted like a wounded animal, retreating from the beating she had received. Destiny never responded. I tried to keep my notes light and upbeat, with a subliminal message that I yearned to hear from her.

"Hey Des, Caroline and Nicole are growing up so fast. I'm sure your boys and little Emily are just as active and happy. Stay in touch. Until next time, Love Rose."

I wrote a little something every day, checked each evening and longed for an answer.

"Des, it's me again. I think about you often and hope you and Ben are doing well. Maybe you could say hello to Glory and River for me. Your parents, too. I miss you all very much."

I wondered if it was better for all of us if I gave up the charade and accepted the effect of the wound I had caused. I needed a diversion and thought about going back to work once Nicole entered pre-school. I tried one last time to contact Destiny, and then I braced myself for rejection.

"Hi Des. I hate to keep bothering you. I'm sure you're busy with your

little ones and the fruit market. That's really wonderful for all of you that River was able to convince the developers to keep the market as part of the subdivision and I'm sure the area has changed immensely. There's so much new building going on in the city as well, and high tech companies are moving into the area by the dozens. It's a whole new world for our children. Remember how content we were eating peanut butter and jelly sandwiches by the creek? Our parents were so trusting that we would come home every day before dark, without a scratch, and we did. I can't imagine letting Caroline and Nicole out of my sight for ten minutes, let alone an entire day."

I paused as I recalled the memory and wished I had been satisfied, like Destiny, with the simplicity of the life our parents tried to provide. I pushed back my chair and read what I had composed. I put myself in her position, deciding it was neither invasive nor aggressive. I needed one more sentence to wrap up what might be the last time I would attempt to stir my friend and prompt a reply.

"I was thinking I might take a little road trip with the girls next spring and come up for a visit. It's been too long since we have seen one another, and I don't want Caroline or Nicole to grow up like I did without knowing th....."

I stopped again. It was beginning to sound pushy and off-putting. I backspaced the last sentence and re-read my note three more times, considering every word and how they might be interpreted. I pushed forward one last time.

"I was thinking I might take a little road trip with the girls next spring and come up for a visit. Let me know if you think that would be a good idea. Love to all, Rose." Send...

"YOU'RE HOME EARLY. What a nice surprise."

Caroline ran to greet her father and Nicole's eyes lit up when she saw him walk towards her, interrupting a tea party with her favorite stuffed animals. She was the spitting image of Andrew, hazel eyes, sandy-blond hair already to her shoulders, and unlike her sister's, straight as a pin. Both girls were tall for their age, hard to escape with parents that were always the tallest in their classes. Once her baby sister started to walk, Caroline thought she made a pretty decent playmate and I felt grateful they entertained each other while I prepared dinner every evening.

Andrew seldom was involved in this scene of domestic bliss, and I welcomed him with a warm embrace. He looked tired. Once I sent the last email to Destiny, a pall was lifted from my shoulders. It felt freeing. At that moment, regardless of whether or not she made an attempt to reach me, I would concentrate on what I had right in front of me, for the sake of Andrew and the girls, but most of all, for myself.

"It's so good to be home at a decent hour."

Andrew returned the embrace before making his way to the leather recliner, and pushed it back as far as it would go. He probably would have fallen asleep right then and there if the girls hadn't dog-piled on him and insisted on a spot on each side of his exhausted body. He inhaled the aroma that enveloped the house, and I saw his lips turn up at the corners into a broad grin.

"That takes me back." He took one more breath as if he could taste the air. "Glory's biscuits. I didn't know you had the recipe...smells so good."

I wiped down the countertops and set the table for four, even though Nicole still used her high chair. By this time we had abandoned the tray so she could be a part of the family dining experience. I mused that I had picked the perfect time to make my mother's delectable biscuits, the ones that graced our table every Sunday, the ones that greeted Andrew the first time we had been introduced. "Just got the urge. Perfect timing."

I wanted to question him and learn why he was home before seven o'clock. I would let him tell me.

The biscuit aroma still lingered past the girl's bedtime. Andrew and I were alone. I sensed he might have something on his mind. He joined me on the couch as I flipped through the mindless game shows I had grown accustomed to as background noise, a filler for the lack of grown-up companionship most evenings.

He brought a plate full of leftover biscuits, already split in half and drenched with honey butter. I hadn't gotten around to mastering the art of preserving fresh fruit like Glory, even though our peach and plum trees gifted us with the bumper crop I hoped for.

"Is everything okay?" I took the half biscuit Andrew offered and shifted into the corner of the couch to make room for him.

"I was about to ask you the same question, Rose. You've been awfully quiet lately."

Did he suspect something, did he notice the lack of communication between my parents and me?"

Did his father call him and mention something? After all, Jacob was his uncle. I'm sure the brothers talked.

"What do you mean? I guess I've seemed quiet to you because you leave early and come home late. We hardly see each other more. I'm plenty talkative during the day. We're both tired by the time you get home," I lied. I had dreaded this conversation for almost a year.

Andrew was always more direct than I was. "Got a phone call from my father..."

So he has heard. He knows. I wonder how long.

"He mentioned that Glory and Jacob didn't talk much about us and the girls lately, and he wondered if everything was okay." The weight of the conversation didn't prevent him from inhaling another biscuit. "Is everything all right? Did something happen that I should know about?"

His question was straightforward and deserved an honest answer. My head tingled and my heartbeat quickened. After I told him everything, the whole ugly truth and how I felt like I had ruined all our lives and robbed the girls of grandparents forever, I retreated deeper into the recesses of the couch and grabbed the largest throw pillow to create a barrier between the two of us. I needed to prepare myself for Andrew's criticism and endure the denunciation to follow. The pillow felt like a protective shield as I braced myself for his reply.

As always, Andrew's tone did not rise past his every day speaking voice. It was not easy to distinguish his moods, especially when he was mad, upset, or concerned. He was the most even-tempered person I had ever met. He found a position in the opposite corner of the couch and shook his head. He bit his lip as if to prevent words from spilling out that he would never be able to retract.

He had a better filter than I did and as much as I feared his reproach, I knew he would choose his words wisely. Much better than I had. He reached behind his head with one arm and leaned into the back of the couch, closed his eyes, and asked, "Why did you do this, Rose?"

It was a simple enough question, but the most difficult of all to answer. "I didn't mean for it to end this way. Do you think I was attempting to lose everything? I wanted some answers." I started to cry, softly, I didn't want to make a scene.

Andrew didn't move. "Answers to what? Is this about River not being your father? Are you still obsessed with that after all these years?"

I recovered my composure but felt helpless as I defended my rationalization about the photograph at Glory's eighteenth birthday party, about her older brother whom no one ever mentioned, about the lack of conversation – not ever explaining why she left her parent's home to live in a commune with twenty other people. I sat up straight.

"Aren't you the least bit curious? I realize it has nothing to do with your side of the family, but I had questions...valid ones, and as remorseful as I feel for my rotten timing, or choice of words, I know there are secrets that were buried with my grandmother."

I kept silent about the possibility of my husband and I being first cousins if River was not my father and Uncle Jacob was. I felt certain the same thought occurred to Andrew as well.

"And you have now succeeded in creating the same chasm between you and Glory as she did with her own mother. You chose to risk all our lives, all our futures, to chase one hairbrained idea to the bitter end to satisfy you, no one else, just you. The rest of us will suffer so you can find an answer to some real or imagined hardship that was perpetrated upon you at birth. No matter what the truth is, River and Glory gave you an amazing life and loved you with all their hearts. Why can't you just leave it at that, Rose? Why can't that be enough?"

He pulled himself up, and looked directly at me for the first time since we had started the conversation. "I hope, for all our sakes, you can fix this one, Rose. You are becoming harder and harder to love."

He couldn't have been more hurtful. I let him move past me, and I watched as he made his way towards the bedroom. His steps were deliberate, slow, and sad. I was sure he would be asleep before I joined him. If he had taken a knife and pierced my heart, it couldn't have caused nearly as much pain as the significance of his words.

I never made it to bed. I curled up into a small ball, covered my body with the warmth of the remaining pillows, and didn't wake up until I heard the happy shrieks of my children, escaped from their room, and the smell of the burnt toast they had prepared on their own.

"You were sleeping, Mommy. I made toast." Caroline greeted me with a grin and strawberry jam dripping from the sides of her mouth. I couldn't help but return the emotion and managed to smile in spite of my heavy heart. I remembered the forlorn look on Andrew's face. He must be feeling the same, or worse, than I was.

"Where's your daddy?"

"He went to work. He said you were very tired. We made breakfast...want some?"

CHAPTER 26

We moved past the conversation, buried it beneath the surface and the idea of repairing the rift between my parents and myself seemed more and more uncertain. Andrew, loyal to his upbringing and steady as a father, husband, and provider, kept our family grounded and brought stability back to our relationship without ever saying another word.

I favored talking things out, hashing out feelings, but I remembered telling myself long ago that he was a man of few words. I knew better than to try to change him, and I did my part to keep our marriage solid and secure. Biscuits were not the only thing I learned how to bake. I discovered the joy of cooking and family dinners. It helped fill the hole that was still there, even though it was never discussed.

I spent mornings, after the house was empty and the girls were ushered out the door with a full belly and a brown sack lunch, checking my emails and teaching myself how to surf the net. Almost every household had a computer, and youngsters knew nothing about dial-ups. Children as young as six years old had their own laptops and cell phones. Andrew and I had made the joint decision to not let our girls have either until they were fourteen and twelve, respectively. We had already diverted the battle in advance, informing them they would get these expensive toys at the same time and would have to wait until we decided they were ready. Andrew had more luck reasoning with them, and they still had a few years to wait.

I didn't want to make another wrong move, a decision I might come to regret, but I was hungry to do something more than be a volunteer classroom aide and stay-at home mom. I felt more like a stay-behind mom. I'd never had the chance to burst forth into the world, the one I couldn't wait to harness when I was a teenager. My degree had gathered dust, and I sensed the date on the diploma, with no work experience in between, would make it difficult to find a job. I put the idea of a career on hold years ago, but wanted more than anything to use my interior designing skills for more than a little girl's bedroom or a home office.

The desktop computer in the family room was fair game to both girls for homework, and they took turns every evening while Andrew and I enjoyed a glass of wine together. During the winter, we would move to the formal living room, and light the fire with the flip of a switch, a convenience neither of us minded. True, we didn't get the scent of fresh logs, or the lingering smell of ash after the last flame had died, but we both agreed we'd had enough of that in our childhoods.

"Rose, wanted to ask you something."

"Funny, I wanted to ask you something, too. You first."

We had ceased being awkward with one another and our relationship had settled into one of best friends, with occasional romantic interludes that satisfied both of us. Every once in a while, if the girls spent the night with friends, or at a week-long camping trip with the summer youth program, we could get frisky with one another and the long-forgotten feelings of lust would surface. I never questioned if this was normal, or had conversations with my girlfriends about my love life, but I suspected it was pretty much the same with everyone else. Twelve years of marriage was a milestone in itself, and I felt lucky to be in one that was as solid as ours.

"Ever think of going back to work? I mean part-time during school hours?"

Had he read my mind?

He took a sip of his Merlot and didn't set aside his wine glass. He took another mouthful before he looked to me for an answer.

"All the time. At least since Nicole started first grade. That was what...four years ago?"

I took my glass of Rosé from the coffee table and savored the flavor. Not so much because my name was Rose, I always preferred the pale red of Rosé or the light salmon tone of Pinot Noir. It didn't take much to make me light headed and the heavier red wines tasted like cough syrup to me.

I was unsure where this conversation was headed and I proceeded with caution. "Is your job okay? Do we need the money?"

"Sweet Rose." Andrew appeared amorous when he responded and did not look concerned. A good sign.

"It's all I can do to get home in time for dinner these days. No, we have so many projects and the firm is going through another hiring phase. I'm not sure how long this ride will last, but the Silicon Valley is bursting at the seams with start-ups and growth of well-established corporations. Everyone needs more room and we have to expand ourselves to remain competitive."

"Must I read between the lines, or are you going to get to the point?" I sounded playful and inquisitive at the same time. "Come on, Handsome." I hadn't called him that in a long time. "Tell me what's going on....did you get a raise?"

Andrew looked excited, a side of him he didn't often expose, and it was fun to watch. "Better, much better." He leaned in and gave me a lingering, sensual kiss before he backed away and announced, "I've been promoted to Senior Partner, and I will be the onsite lead architect for the Palo Alto Division. We're in the process of closing escrow on an older, dated office building that will house thirty full-time employees. Gonna be much different than working in a high-rise, but not having to battle traffic and congestion every day appeals to me."

"Are you going to tell me what this has to do with me, or not? Please, get on with it." I was enjoying the banter, the playful atmosphere was not lost on me, but I was anxious to hear what else he had to say.

"Okay, Rose, this is where you come in." He took another sip of wine and carefully placed it back on the table. He was killing me. "I hired a design firm to re-model the office interiors. They're as slammed as the architects with this building boom, and they're looking to bring on additional staff to complete this project. Probably others, too. I told them you had your degree in Interior Design and asked if they might consider you for an interview. Hope you don't mind." He searched my face.

My reaction could have gone either way, thrilled or

petrified. I felt a little of both, and I wanted nothing more than to call Glory.

OF COURSE, I NEVER CALLED Glory. I couldn't. Her silence was her message to me that she didn't want to be disturbed or contacted, now or in the future. I forced myself to stop searching the emails every morning for a glimmer of hope from Destiny. I kept up with life at the commune through Andrew's parents.

They didn't get together often, from what I had been told, and they shared little with me or Andrew. They lived too far from each other and kept in touch mostly by phone calls and letters. Our parent's generation was loathe to relinquish letter writing and snail mail. It would have been nice to know if Glory or River ever asked about me, or if they divulged to Aunt Fern and Uncle Jacob the reason we no longer spoke, but those questions were off limits.

At least Caroline and Nicole had one set of grandparents that were very much in their lives. After the first couple years, Caroline stopped asking about Papa altogether. I assumed she no longer remembered what he looked like or knew who he was.

I THRIVED ON WORKING, and so brushing up on my skills was not as hard as I thought it would be. Most of my co-workers were ten years younger, fresh-faced and recent graduates of top-notch universities.

The men were mostly gay, attracted to the industry by

their artistic abilities and keen eye for color and fashion. The young women were bold and brash. You could tell they were trying to get ahead in their profession quickly. No one had the patience once described as a virtue, and a slow climb up the ladder was no longer the norm. If any of these "kids", as I called them, were around three years from their date of hire, it would be unusual.

Loyalty in the workplace had been replaced by a race to the finish by any means possible. A whole new generation under the age of twenty-five flooded the workplace, making names for themselves and salaries to match. Money flowed like water, and this new group of young people both irritated and astounded me.

As for myself, I was content to be a part of the effort, with easy hours and enough influence within the team to make me feel valuable. I began to wonder less and less about River and Glory, and I welcomed work as the perfect distraction.

CHAPTER 27

My phone never rang after eight o'clock at night. I was jarred from my sleep by the loud chiming noises I had set as my ring tone. I pressed the center button to illuminate the time. Almost eleven. Andrew slept deeply beside me, and not even the incessant ring could rouse him. I was glad for that, but a bit nervous when I answered and wondered who would call me at such a late hour.

I answered, hesitantly. "Hello?" *Please, don't let it be bad news.*

I recognized the voice on the other end. "I'm so sorry, Rose. I know it's late. It's Betsy."

I don't think Betsy ever slept and probably earned her gray hair and deep wrinkles through decades of managing one of the most revered design houses in Northern California. Her father had started the business before her birth. Inheriting the firm he had built from scratch, along with a work ethic that was well known in the industry, left her no time for marriage or family. All she did was work and I admired her for devotion and kindness to all of her employees.

"Is something wrong, Betsy?" I couldn't imagine why she

might be calling me. I was a part-time employee, and we seldom spoke to each other at the office. Most of my ideas were funneled to her through my superior, Jack Chambers, young, recently divorced, and father of a two-year old son.

I eased myself out of bed and grabbed my robe. The house was freezing, but we never slept with the heat on. We preferred the warmth of a good down comforter. Popping out of bed before morning was not something I was used to. I wrapped myself tight in the flannel and made my way to the kitchen to prevent waking Andrew.

"What does your schedule look like the day after tomorrow?" Betsy didn't waste any time.

"Thursday?" I glanced at the family calendar posted on the wall by the refrigerator.

"Soccer practice for Caroline and dance lesson for Nicole. Both late afternoon."

"Friday?"

"Birthday party for one of their little friend's in the cul-de-sac."

Oh crap, I forgot all about it. I still have to pick up a present...two of them. One from Caroline, one from Nicole.

"Can you get someone to cover you for those appointments?"

Appointments...I guess everything that is calendared in is an appointment to Betsy, even when children are involved.

"I need someone on your team to fill in for Trevor. He's come down with the flu, and he was supposed to accompany Jack to LA on Thursday. It wouldn't look good if I sent one designer instead of the two I promised for the pitch. Jack suggested you. He said you know more than any of the other team members, and you have an air of maturity about you. We need a solid, well-rounded and articulate team mate."

Her comments made me feel old. I was barely in my thirty's and already being referred to as 'mature.' "Will I have enough time to prepare?"

"Jack says you know enough, and he will fill you in tomorrow. Can you stay a little late if necessary?"

I tried to think on my feet. I didn't want to wake Andrew, but I knew Betsy was waiting for an answer. "Can I say a tentative yes? I need to talk to Andrew. I need to make arrangements for the girls."

"I'll take that as a 'yes'. Thank you, Rose. Now we can both get some sleep."

Maybe she slept, but I tossed and turned all night. I also wondered what I had just gotten myself into.

"GLAD YOU WERE ABLE to get everything covered, Rose."

We squeezed ourselves into the last two seats in the waiting area, an hour before take-off, for our early morning flight from San Francisco Airport to Burbank. Betsy hired a driver for us. I was picked up first, farthest distance from the airport, and wasn't used to waking at 4:00 a.m. to prepare for anything, let alone a flight from one part of the state to the other.

Southern California may as well have been New York City. I had never been, didn't know anyone who lived there or anything about it past the entertainment shows I occasionally watched with self-serving celebrities and unfamiliar names. I was out of touch with anything remotely related to Hollywood, music, or the movies.

Caroline and Nicole rattled off names at the dinner table and downloaded pictures of their favorite pre-teen singers, but I couldn't relate. It was far removed from my upbringing with no TV. We entertained ourselves by playing board games that we picked up from Goodwill for fifty cents, and we felt fortunate if all the pieces were included. I stuffed down the memories every time they started to surface. My girls would never know the simple communal upbringing of their mother.

Our prospective clients, an upscale financial advisor firm, represented some of the wealthiest members of the community. Basketball players, movie stars, rock idols. With new entries in the industry every day, and more competition from younger, less established companies, they needed a make-over to impress their rivals and retain their most successful employees.

They had the manpower, but their look was 1990. The new catchphrase was "wow factor", even though that didn't necessarily translate to the best design. If I was the likely nominee to replace Trevor on this trip, it was only because Jack was five years my junior and had a grip on trends and colors. Maybe there was a method to Betsy's madness and the reason why she wanted to send me as Jack's wingman – the responsible female.

Betsy made sure we had the most sumptuous accommodations. Our firm could afford it. It was her first venture out of Northern California and she wanted to take us to the next level, break out of the comfort zone created by her father. It was the only way she would be able to survive a throng of new start-up design houses waiting to dethrone her. She was banking on our ability to seal the deal.

We were the last design team to interview. Our props, sent ahead the day before, were delivered well in advance of our appointment. Everything was ready when we arrived by cab. She made it easy for us by arranging for a courier to take our bags to the hotel and check us in. One less thing to worry about. Everything was on the line for her, but I felt like I was along for the ride.

For all my imagination and sometimes obsessive behavior, one thing I never paid much attention to was my looks. The last time I decided to change anything about myself was back in college, when Destiny took me for a complete makeover and I risked what little self-esteem I had to impress Andrew with a daring new haircut. He loved it, so did I. It eventually grew out, along with the highlights, and I never bothered much beyond a simple trim of the ends.

I found a length that worked, both for ease of care and what I thought was the most flattering, right below my shoulder blades. I kept my chestnut waves parted in the middle, the same length all around my head, and depending on the weather, I either pulled it back into a ponytail, or let it flow freely, which meant I was constantly flicking it out of my eyes.

For this trip, I kept it out of my face to ensure whoever I spoke to knew I had nothing to hide. Andrew's one piece of advice before I left the house was, "be direct, smile, look people in the eye when you're talking, don't interrupt, and most of all listen. Knock 'em dead, my love. I'm proud of you."

I didn't have time to be nervous, and I was in control. It was the first time I had left the girls, but they were old enough. Hard for me to believe Caroline was almost ready for middle school and Nicole was two short years behind. The mother-daughter battles I had read about had yet to visit our household, but I armed myself with mental notes and words of wisdom I was ready to use the first time one of them slammed a door in my face, or yelled, "You're not the boss of me and all my friend's parents let them do it!"

I couldn't recall giving Glory or River this type of grief, but I pretty much ran my own show and did whatever I wanted in those days. I was also a bit of a recluse and didn't hang out with any particular crowd. Peer pressure was not front and center in our home, but I always wondered if it was a different scene at Destiny's house. Maybe Uncle Jacob and Aunt Fern had their hands full behind closed doors.

"YOU BLEW THEM AWAY, Rose. Where did you come up with those ideas? They were genius! A traditional, on-trend assortment of old and new designs in one space? Where have you been hiding? I knew you were talented, but I've never seen you speak up like that before."

"Well, you must have had some idea if you asked for me specifically."

Jack let his hand brush across my thigh. The limo partition, coated with a thick shield of black-out film, was rolled up to obscure activity in the back seat.

I felt trapped, like a junkyard dog captured and thrown into the back of an animal control vehicle. I had no means of escape from the fast-moving ride in a sea of rush hour traffic. I was terrified something awful was about to happen.

I'm sure my voice sounded panicked. I don't know what he expected. Did he think I would be a willing participant? Had this younger man, newly divorced with a small child, caused the demise of his own marriage? Was he out trolling for a good time at every opportunity? Was this how unscrupulous scum made it to the top?

Calm down. You can handle this. Take control. If he doesn't back off, you can bang the shit out of the window and get the driver's attention. Jack won't let it get that far. He'd better not.

I tried my best to keep an even timbre in my voice and removed his hand from my thigh. It felt dirty from his touch. I let it drop with a resolute motion onto the seat between us, and I looked straight ahead. "Don't go there, Jack. I'm not available." I longed for my husband and couldn't believe the position I had found myself in.

"You sure? I thought I got some kind of signal back there in the board room." He started to move his hand again.

I knocked it away, this time with more force.

"Your radar is flawed."

I wanted to call him a swine, a jerk, an idiot, and worse, but I also didn't want to enrage him or puncture his ego so he would try to retaliate.

Keep your cool. "I'm sorry if you think I sent up a flag. I was direct, smiled, looked people in the eye when I spoke, didn't interrupt, and most of all, listened." Andrew would have been proud.

I won the battle. Jack backed off, but not before muttering under his breath, "You don't know what you're missing."

The last word was important to him, and he could have it.

We sat in silence all the way to the hotel. I didn't wait for the limo driver to open my door. I practically flew out of the car, the door left open wide.

I approached the front desk to get my key and whispered to the desk clerk, "Please change my room to a lower level closest to lobby." I didn't want to take any chances of running into Jack later in the evening, and I didn't care if the hotel charged extra for storing my suitcase in the original room. If anyone said anything, I would pay any overage out of my own paycheck.

I called Betsy as soon as I got to my room. I told her I felt sick to my stomach, probably had the same flu as Trevor, and thought I should get back home as soon as possible. I told her I would be making a change in my reservation and leaving first thing in the morning, instead of staying on with Jack one more day.

"I'm sorry you're not feeling well, Rose. Of course, come home early. Jack can finish up the little left to be done on his own." For all I knew, she could have read between the lines. My voice sounded terse and shaky.

"By the way Rose, might as well tell you while I have you on the phone. I was going to call Jack later tonight, but since I have your undivided attention, we no longer have prospective clients...they're now *our* clients. They loved the pitch and fell in love with you. Congratulations. We'll talk next week."

I thanked her and started to hang up the phone.

"And Rose, feel better."

For her lack of maternal instincts and never having experienced motherhood, Betsy had a soft, caring heart. I wondered if she ever regretted her choice to remain single, or if she'd had a choice. Maybe it just happened. I would give her my notice on Monday.

CHAPTER 28

I didn't explain to Andrew why I returned earlier than planned. He and the girls were just happy to have me home, and I had never felt such relief in my life. I dodged what could have been a most disastrous event if I had not been able to fend off Jack's advances.

What did I know about business trips? Why did I think I could masquerade as a professional, with street smarts and a knack for climbing a ladder at any cost? I wanted something to do during the day when Caroline and Nicole were at school and Andrew was at the office. I never bargained for the politics or harassment that were part and parcel of a career. It was moving too quickly for me.

I flashed on my mother, her choice to pursue a simple, pure, and untainted lifestyle. That's how she raised me, and it was becoming more and more apparent to me that my values were not so different from hers.

With the downtime Andrew had prepared for, we took advantage of the pause in our hectic schedule. We packed up the girls on Saturday morning and headed to Lake Tahoe, a welcome respite from the intense activity of the city.

"Do we have to bring our homework?" Caroline sounded

hopeful as she rushed to cram her backpack with tennis shoes, shorts, and lightweight sweatshirts.

"Bring it along. You can do it in the car."

Sighs of resignation were audible, but both Andrew and I ignored them. We tried to get used to pre-teen grumblings and objections. It was an everyday occurrence and I tried to remember if I had ever been that difficult. Surely, I told myself, I was the perfect child. A little distant sometimes, an over-active imagination, but I couldn't recall challenging my parent's decisions or requests. There weren't as many distractions, that's for sure. What I once felt was the most boring life on the planet was beginning to look idyllic compared to all the noise and commotion that surrounded us every day.

I WALKED OUT OF MY meeting with Betsy on Monday morning, not quite certain what had transpired. I was caught off guard and my plan to submit my two-week notice was derailed before I had a chance to explain. I decided not to mention Jack, or the real reason I was leaving. I planned to highlight the fact that I needed to spend more time at home, the girls were still too young to be on their own, even for an hour after school, and I planned to shelve the idea of a career until they were both in high school. My mental notes were well scripted, and I felt she would understand.

"Sit down, Rose. I hope you're feeling better. You look wonderful, relaxed."

Don't say anything about your weekend in Tahoe. Best to let her think it was the flu that prompted your early return from LA.

"Tea?" Her desk was set with an assortment of expensive

teas, loose instead of bagged, and the aroma was heavenly. The thermal, stainless carafe was set with hot water, two liters, enough for re-fills all day long.

"Tea does sound good. Thank you." I craned my neck to view the array more closely. "Peppermint."

"Easy on the stomach, in case you're still not feeling well."

Did she know something, or was she intuitive? I guessed she was my mother's age. This scene reminded me of coffee on the porch, tea by the fire, treasured moments Glory and I shared with those old, brightly colored mugs that somehow made it through season after season of dishwashing and heavy handling. I wondered if they were still around or if she thought of me when she used them.

"You were brilliant in LA, Rose." Betsy handed me the piping hot mug of peppermint tea, infused to perfection with the right balance of aged tea leaves and flavor.

"I've never been much of a tea drinker. On rare occasions." I drew in the fragrance of the mint before taking the first sip. "This might change my mind."

I felt soothed and ready to proceed, I would fill Betsy in on the meeting, finish our conversation, divulge my plans, and exit.

Betsy had a rehearsed speech, as well. I waited for her to say what was on her mind. She continued to praise my performance in the board room, explaining that everyone was impressed with my attention to detail and vision. None of the other candidates presented ideas that would create the long-lasting design model I proposed. Instead, they had offered over-used suggestions and popular colors, textures, and ideas that would be outdated within three years. Jack was there, as well, and had an obvious connection to the team, but Betsy seemed solely concerned with my performance.

"I spoke with Jack after I hung up with you. I gave you credit for your ideas and presentation and mentioned we had won the contract based on your handling of the group and your mature approach to a new design model."

"What did he say? Anything?"

I looked for a tell-tale sign that he might have told her something, or tried to put a spin on a story before I had a chance to talk with her. Little did he know that I had no plans to tell Betsy anything, or Andrew, and I planned to quit my job as soon as I got back into the office on Monday. My grip on the mug tightened.

"He congratulated us, you, me, the team. With his next breath, he said he quit, and wouldn't return to work. He's coming by later this afternoon to pick up his personal items from his desk and get his final paycheck."

My vise-like grip on the cup of tea relaxed, the surprised expression on my face obvious. It was the right reaction so as not to encourage questions from this nice lady, my soon to be ex-boss. I felt overwhelming relief. At the same time, I felt terrible, knowing I was about to give Betsy my resignation as well. There were six of us on the team. I was certain someone would be left to carry the torch and finish the project in LA. Before I could open my mouth, she rushed to finish her thoughts.

"I want you to head up the team, Rose. You may not have the years of work experience under your belt, but you're poised, calm, and down-to-earth. You're the only employee I have that, like me, thinks that less is sometimes more, and the wheel doesn't always have to be reinvented to be progressive. Are you interested in the position, Rose? I could really use you to complete this project, and I have no doubt our clients in LA are looking forward to working with you."

She was steady as a rock. I knew if I declined the offer, this jewel in her crown, this opportunity to break out of the mold created by her father would be jeopardized. I also knew that the LA design would probably never materialize if Jack and I both walked out on her. I wanted to make the right choice for Betsy, myself, Andrew and the girls. I could tell Betsy was anxious for an answer, and I had seconds to decide.

Thoughts raced and I verbalized the first concrete idea that jumped into my head. "I'm flattered, Betsy. I have to admit this conversation is not at all what I had envisioned when I came in this morning. Can I request one thing...well, maybe two...maybe more." I shot her a weak smile. "I'm thinking on my feet here...I have a lot to consider. Most importantly, I have to run it by Andrew. I know he thinks the world of you or he never would have suggested an interview last year, but I still want his blessing."

"It's refreshing to see a relationship where a couple talks about their decisions and how they affect each other."

If she only knew. I pushed that thought away. It cropped up at the most inopportune times.

"No business trips unless Andrew and the girls are allowed to accompany me."

"No problem." Betsy nodded in agreement. "There's lots of things for families to do in LA. I agree wholeheartedly and support your desire to bring them along. Most of the time, we'll be telecommuting. I can't see any reason to go down South more than once or twice during the project. The contract calls for six months and most of the day-to-day creations will take place in this office. You can always send a team member down for a few days if something comes up, but I want you to be the lead designer. Anything else?"

I stammered. My mind raced with all the possible scenarios

and I didn't want to promise anything I couldn't deliver. "Can I still maintain my part-time status?" I knew it was a long shot, but I couldn't see myself being gone all day and working long hours, absent from home and our growing girls.

Betsy took a few moments to consider.

"Compromise?" She suggested.

"How so?"

The conversation moved quickly from there as Betsy continued. "Work from home on Mondays and Fridays, no more than eight hours a day Tuesday through Thursday and return to part-time when the LA project is complete."

I could tell it was her best offer. She waited for my response. I felt overwhelmed by a decision that would affect all of us, but at the same time proud that I had considered those around me. My motives were unselfish.

I hadn't realized until that moment how tense my body had become. My shoulders relaxed with her suggestion. It sounded like a perfect solution, and Andrew would probably agree. I could take this one home to him. "I accept."

I set my empty mug on the edge of the desk and smiled. I thanked her for her faith in my abilities, pushed back my chair, and headed for the door. I could smell the peppermint that lingered in the air as I closed it behind me.

My self-confidence soared even as I wondered, *What just happened in there?*

CHAPTER 29

I had been naïve. Andrew had been more accurate when he proposed that, even though I had an agreement to work on much of the project from home, my weekends would not always be free and there would be fires to douse throughout the entire project. "Being team leader is far different than being part of the team. I'm just saying...prepare yourself. I've been at this grind for a lot longer than you, my love."

I was sure he was wrong and sought his blessing. That's all I needed to convince myself that I had made the right choice.

Caroline and Nicole thought it was a grand idea. They told me a working mother was far more exciting than one who stayed home all day, cleaned the house and cooked dinner. I don't know where they got that idea. Perhaps they missed the part where I also went to the grocery store, did the laundry, chauffeured them back and forth to sports and dance practices, took them to doctor appointments and baked for the PTA fundraisers. But if they didn't mind the temporary shift in the household, neither did I.

"All the other kids have their own laptops and cell phones."

And there it was, the first push back from my youngest daughter. Nicole was already working it, taking advantage of my vulnerable position and guilt for leaving them with a nanny three days a week. At least she wasn't arguing about unchaperoned camping trips or demanding she be able to stay out until 1:00 in the morning...yet. How did she get so good – so young? They didn't need to know that their father and I had already made the decision earlier and her whining had no impact whatsoever. Andrew and I glanced at each other and smiled.

We all got new laptops, new cell phones, and an upgraded internet contract that provided uninterrupted service and connectivity. I didn't stop to think if we needed all of these high-tech gadgets. None of us needed it, but it was expected that every household and office be equipped with the latest and greatest devices meant to keep our worlds running smoothly, on-time, in step, modernized.

I felt smothered by all the expectations and the mental and physical clutter created by too much stuff meant to make our lives easier, which actually made it harder. Actually, most days, it was exhausting. I suppressed the belief that we were becoming members of a wasteful society and that River and Glory might have been right. I would never admit it to Andrew, but I was beginning to wonder what my life would have been like if I had never left the commune. Certainly there would have been no Andrew, and I couldn't imagine my life without him or my girls.

On Tuesdays, I arrived at the office early to make up for the long break away from the rest of the team. I managed to maintain my original plan to stay home Friday through Monday, but it often delayed decisions and hands-on approval. I didn't want to impede the momentum or the accuracy our clients expected from us. We reached the tail end of our contract period for our LA project. Except for a few day trips I took on my own, most of our meetings were accomplished through a series of weekly conference calls and face-time reviews.

A stack of mail always greeted me on Tuesday mornings, part of the reason I arrived early. Most of it was junk, and for all the talk of saving trees and reducing paper waste, it arrived every day and I needed at least an hour to sort through the pile. A thick, legal-sized envelope caught my eye. I looked at the postmark first, Washington, the sender second. Uncle Jacob.

IT HAD BEEN TEN YEARS...ten long years...since I'd created a falling-out so damaging, so thoughtless, so cruel.

What would I find once I pried open the envelope? Would my life be up-ended again? What terrible news would I find to destroy the semblance of normalcy I had fought so hard to create?

My guilt had followed me like a lost puppy, but I did my best to accept it. It didn't stop me from wondering every day what my life, our lives, might have been like if I had kept quiet.

I wanted to rip into the contents right away. It felt squishy, and I couldn't tell what might be inside. Instead of forcing open the small package, I grabbed a letter opener and let it slice across the top, careful not to damage the return address.

Along with a letter, neatly folded in thirds, was a baggy that contained a paper towel, concealing something that Uncle Jacob wanted to either preserve or protect. I set the plastic to one side and, with a sinking feeling, unfolded the letter.

Dear Rose,

I hope this letter will not upset you. My intention is to answer some of your questions and clear up any misgivings you may have harbored throughout your life. Your parents, Fern, and I always knew you had an active imagination and a profound ability to observe everything that went on around you. Even at a young age you seemed to provide yourself with an escape hatch into a different world and couldn't wait to burst free from the confines of the commune. I want you to know there is some truth in what you have long suspected, but the decision to find further proof will be up to you.

My hands started to shake, and I wasn't sure I wanted to know what came next. I realized from the first sentence that he knew about my conversation with Glory. They all did. I was certain of that now. I glanced at my watch...still early...I expected no interruptions for at least thirty minutes.

Our generation was far different than anything you can imagine. Our parents were products of World War II, the Vietnam War was winding down, and we had sustained the loss of tens of thousands of our own brothers, sisters, uncles, aunts, and friends because of that conflict. Every one of my classmates was personally affected, and we all knew someone who had perished. River and I were spared from the draft as we weren't quite old enough to serve in the late sixties at the height of the fighting. But San Francisco was a mecca for hippies, coffee shops, peace rallies, love-ins and free love.

I won't go into details and no one else is aware I am sharing this information with you, but it breaks my heart that you and your parents have not spoken in all these years, and I might very well have contributed to your sorrow. Along with a dozen other friends, we chose the communal lifestyle, which obviously did not appeal to you. We all understood your choice to find a more suitable life for yourself. I hope you have found that with Andrew and your daughters.

I have enclosed what you will need for a DNA sample that you can use to answer the question that has haunted you for most of your life, or reject it in favor of realizing you are who you are, no matter what the answer might reveal. There are plusses and minuses in knowing and not knowing, and if your desire is such, I'm sure there is a lab that will accommodate your request.

Uncle Jacob was validating my doubts, the answer was at hand if I chose, and I felt like I was going to throw up. It was all I could do to get to the bottom of the letter. I had an idea what the plastic bag might contain.

Before I close, I have one more piece of information to disclose, but one that will calm your heart should you decide to follow this trail to the end. It is my hope you will not share any of this communication with Andrew, not this part at least, because he has neither been told nor ever questioned this situation. Unlike you, he is not the curious type, and even if he had speculated in his mind, he never let on and his parents and I assume he has no knowledge that he is adopted.

I almost dropped the letter and fumbled to regain my composure. That's why his parents were married for five years before he came along. How could he not know? Why did everyone keep secrets? Where is the truth...the God damned truth?

Not long after his first birthday, his mother became pregnant with his younger sister, and the second one followed a few years later. I'm told that happens and is not unusual. I trust this admission will remain between us. It will not serve any good purpose to pursue Andrew's adoption any further, and I tell you only because, not knowing what you might find with a DNA test, I want you to be assured that he is not your cousin. No matter what happens, you are not related by blood. I hope that will bring you some peace at this difficult moment.

Beyond all of this, I hope you have found a life that has suited your personality and your girls are growing up intelligent, beautiful, and strong...just like their mother. Be well, Rose.

With Love Always,

Uncle Jacob

P.S. Your mother misses you.

My heart dropped, then fluttered with anticipation. I reached for the baggy, unzipped the fastener and placed the paper towel in front of me. I unwrapped the folds to reveal three strands of hair, roots intact, my answer to the past and to the future.

What I would do with this confession? The answers to all of my questions remained to be seen.

THE FAINT TAP ON MY OFFICE DOOR intruded on my thoughts. I glanced at my watch – almost seven-thirty. By eight o'clock, the office would come alive with the hum of productive thoughts, meetings, and jovial encounters in the employee kitchen. Betsy poked her head inside. "I saw the light under the door. You're the first one here. Isn't it a bit early?"

When she saw me take the envelope and jerk open my desk drawer, I wondered if she thought I was stealing company secrets. I squared my shoulders and continued to rustle through the stack of unopened mail. "Oh, you know me. Tuesdays take extra time to sort through all this junk...wanted to clear my desk before the meeting."

She knew something was not right. I could tell. The slight arch of her eyebrow, almost undetectable, was not lost on me. Or maybe I was feeling paranoid.

"You look pale, Rose."

I didn't doubt all color had drained from my face after reading Uncle Jacob's letter.

"You've been working long hours, but we're at the finish line with our LA clients. I'll make sure we have a fresh pot of peppermint tea at the meeting." She was gone before I could mumble another word.

I retrieved the letter from the drawer, hidden in haste, and decided to put it into the bottom portion of the desk with a locked file. I had been served up on a silver platter the answer I had searched for my whole life. For all my preparation and wishful thinking, I had no idea what to do next.

CHAPTER 30

It was a long day. Not only because I couldn't concentrate, but because there were vital demands from our client that required swift action. The early morning meeting dragged on until noon over a situation I felt didn't warrant hours of discussion. Namely, paint or wallpaper?

"It doesn't have to be your grandmother's wallpaper," I argued, "but spa colors and light gray walls have been over-used. It will be dated before the paint dries. Why not take a bold step and bring back wallpaper into the twenty-first century? Maybe a grasscloth in bold marine blue as a backdrop." I was merely mouthing concerns and ideas while everyone else started to yawn. "Good wallpaper is expensive, but we still have money in the budget."

I by-passed the objections and reached for the phone. "We can settle this in one call."

While I waited to be connected to my contact in LA, I brought up photos on the forty-two-inch screen of never-before-seen wallpaper designs, ecologically sound and made from bamboo and hemp. All the illegal materials my parents had praised were making a popular comeback. I wondered how they might react if they knew I was singing the praises of these sustainable products in the modern world. I assured myself that they would probably laugh.

A slight smile creased my face as I continued the conversation with my Los Angeles co-worker. "Wallpaper or paint? Any preference?"

My contact on the other end of the phone didn't hesitate. "I trust your judgment. My boss loves everything you've done so far. I'm not going to struggle to make a decision as minor as this one. If we don't like what you put on the walls, it's an easy fix, right?"

"Correct. If you aren't happy with our choices, it's a simple remedy. We'll take care of it, no charge." I looked in Betsy's direction for her approval and she gave me a silent, but enthusiastic, thumbs up. "We'll send you something in writing by tomorrow."

"Now, that's a problem solver," said Betsy. "Take note everyone."

If she only knew.

ANDREW AND THE GIRLS HAD no challenges fending for themselves that night. I couldn't go home to their smiling faces or pretend I had not just gotten the shock of my life. I needed a few hours between dinner and bedtime so I wouldn't be forced to make conversation with any of them.

I struggled with my decision throughout the day...do I really want to know? Why did it take so long for someone to reach out and notice that maybe I was also caught in the crossfire of this deception and my pain was as real as theirs?

How did Uncle Jacob know where I worked...easy enough to find out, I suppose...he talked to his brother.

My thoughts remained jumbled all day long, but I managed to make it through to the end. Betsy left early. I was relieved. I did, too.

I left the letter and its contents behind, safe in a locked drawer. I packed my laptop and looked for the least populated coffee house on the way home. I was anxious to hook up to a WiFi connection and research the possibilities of DNA testing. Tremendous strides had been made. Maybe the first decade of the twenty-first century would provide some answers. Along with the specific samples necessary to prove paternity, a blood sample, cheek swab, or strand of hair with roots and follicle attached – *bingo* – were cautionary examples of how people's lives were changed...forever.

"The test is completely definitive," claimed one diagnostic lab.

I barely noticed the time, and I hadn't touched my bran muffin or the over-priced, decaf coffee I had purchased to secure my spot at a corner table. I absorbed the contents of the information from several websites. I hadn't made up my mind one way or another, whether I would pursue the test or burn the samples Uncle Jacob had sent,

I exited out after reading one profound line, **"DNA Doesn't Make a Father."** The words jumped off the page. I was getting closer to making a decision, but before I closed this chapter of my life, I wanted to see my mother. I sensed she wanted to see me.

Three hours...I didn't realize how long I had been sitting there. I had avoided the watchful eye of the barista every time she walked by with a damp towel, or made overt rustling noises as she emptied the trash. I was absorbed but wanted to get home before Andrew would question my whereabouts. Before shutting down my laptop, I pulled up my email and dashed off a note to Destiny. She was the first person who entered my mind and the only one who might want to coordinate a visit with Glory. It was worth a try.

Hi Destiny,

It's been far too long and I only have myself to blame for not reaching out sooner. Without going into detail, I would like to know if you would take a message to Glory for me. Tell her I would like to see her, perhaps next month. I miss her, always have. I hope I am not intruding on your space or asking something of you that you are uncomfortable relating. I'm sure, over the years, Glory, River, or your parents have given you the details of what went wrong so many years ago. I have attached a picture of Caroline, Nicole, Andrew and myself when we were at Tahoe last year. Maybe she would like to see it. I would like nothing more than to visit with you and your family as well if you think that would be a good idea. Please get back to me.

Love,

Rose

I slapped the laptop shut, unplugged the portable charger, and sent a quick text to Andrew to let him know I was on my way home. I tucked a $20 bill in the tip jar.

ANDREW DIDN'T QUESTION ME or look overly concerned when I got home. It was almost eight o'clock. Uncle Jacob was right about one thing. My husband was not the curious type. Plus, I hadn't given him any reason to worry. He looked up from his newspaper and smiled. "Got your text. Thanks for letting me know." If those words had spilled from the mouths of one of our daughters, it would have been laced with sarcasm, but with Andrew, it was cut and dried, simple, straightforward. He received my message, and he was happy that I'd let him know. Period. He made it all look so easy, while I still questioned every possible nuance, conversation, and bump in the road as a mountain instead of a hill.

"Girls around?"

Andrew didn't look up from the paper and motioned towards the stairs. "They're upstairs finishing their homework. I told them you'd be late."

I dropped my laptop on the front entry table that had become the catch-all for junk mail and bills. I kicked off my shoes and rubbed my feet. All of me was tired.

"I'll be right back down. I want to say goodnight to Caroline and Nicole." I dragged myself up the stairs with the help of the handrail. I had to tell Andrew about the letter from Uncle Jacob. The secrets stopped here, whether he was ready for it or not.

At the top of the stairs, I turned around and looked back at my handsome husband, oblivious, unaware. In a voice loud enough to hear from the distance between us, I said, "We need to talk."

Andrew looked up from the article, until this moment too engrossed to notice the expression on my face or the hint of apprehension in my voice.

"YOU'RE SO GOOD WITH THE GIRLS, Andrew. You always have been. I've spent too many hours away from them...from you...I don't know how other mothers do this."

"Maybe they don't." He patted the empty space beside him, an invitation to sit down. "Is that what you wanted to talk to me about? I ran into Betsy today at the bank, and she said she was looking for a permanent, full-time designer. She had other clients waiting in line once you were finished with the LA job."

Andrew had just handed me the perfect opportunity to divert the conversation, but I had steeled myself to be honest with my husband, lay it all out on the table, and hear his thoughts...or maybe his disapproval. I planned to move forward with the DNA test. My mind wasn't made up yet as to how I might accomplish it, or when it might happen, but I was resolute with my quest and needed the answer.

"No," I faltered. I was surprised to hear this. Betsy hadn't said anything to me and, after the meeting, nothing had been mentioned. "We were both too busy today, big meeting, too much happening. She never said a word."

"Would you accept it if she offered? I think...."

We were totally off track, and whether I accepted or didn't accept a full-time position with Betsy's firm was the farthest thing from my mind. I stopped him in mid-sentence and lowered my head so I didn't have to look him in the eye. I had prepared myself for an eruption, even though Andrew never swore and seldom raised his voice. I steadied myself and carefully chose my words. I had learned a few things about unfiltered comments and thoughtless accusations.

"I got a letter today at the office...from Uncle Jacob." I rushed to finish my thoughts so I wouldn't be interrupted. "He told me my misgivings were not unfounded, but he didn't have the answers. He included three strands of his hair for DNA testing if I wanted to move ahead with knowing the truth."

Andrew slowly exhaled. I could tell he had been holding his breath, waiting for the shoe to drop. He stared at the ceiling with a look of resignation. I could tell the difference with him between disappointment and acceptance. It was the same thing he did when picking his battles with our girls. Some things just weren't worth fighting over. His body slumped further into the couch, and he hunched forward.

He closed his eyes and chose his words. "I never expected you to let this go, Rose, and I thank you for including me. Whatever your decision, I know I won't be able to stop you. I only ask one thing." His eyes slowly opened and he rolled his head in my direction. "Don't tell the girls. They don't need to know any of this, and it will serve no useful purpose. Keep them out of this." The timbre of his voice changed. "Promise me, Rose?"

For the moment, I could agree. I believed he had their best interest at heart, and so did I. That's why I wondered if I could keep my promise if I found out a truth that needed to be shared. "Yes, Andrew, I promise."

CHAPTER 31

It was only a week, but it felt like years. I did my best not to get distracted at work or home, but I checked daily, sometimes ten times, for a response from Destiny. I linked my email to my phone, carried my laptop everywhere, and restrained myself from crossing the line from longing to obsession. I briefly encountered Betsy in the hall when I arrived Tuesday morning, early as always to sort through the clutter and disorder of unopened mail.

"Have time for tea this afternoon, Rose? My office.... noonish?"

Since Andrew mentioned he had run into her the week before, I wasn't surprised at her invitation even though I responded like I was. "Great, love to, Betsy. It will give me time to round up the final invoices and sort through all this mail."

She was a nice woman. I pondered how I would react when she offered me the job, assuming that's what the meeting was about. It seemed logical with the success of my first, full-fledged assignment that her offer would be forthcoming. My head raced with the thought that I might be presented an opportunity to compete with some of the best designers in the city, but also one that would leave me even less time with my family. I felt grateful for Andrew's heads up, and I wrestled with the decision before I was even offered the job.

My phone was flashing in the background. I silenced all the notifications during work, but there was always one or more annoying, blinking light to distract me. Most of it was unimportant, requests for an urgent response from people I had never heard of, my name passed from one sales list to the next. I reminded myself that, no matter how much I hated all the technological advances of the twenty-first century, it was either jump on board or go live in a cave...or a commune. Annoyed, I grabbed the phone. The email icon was lit up with one message.

I tapped the envelope icon on the screen. One message, unread, was highlighted. Sender...Destiny. If I had stopped to consider what her message might contain, I would have never opened it. I hit the unopened email subject line as fast as I could steady the phone in my hand.

Hello Rose,

It's hard to know where to start, trying to pretend that we haven't seen each other in ten years and none of this ever happened. Jacob's brother has managed to stay in touch with us and let us know that you are all fine. It's nice that your girls have one set of grandparents they can see for holidays and special occasions and that Andrew is still close to his family. Like mine, they are growing up fast and are quite beautiful.

I tried to stuff my feelings. Was I the only one who felt

not all of this was my fault? Was everyone else so passive that they never saw the truth? Maybe I was the only one who cared. Maybe it mattered only to me.

I saw there wasn't much more to the email and raced through it. My eyes stung as I continued. Had Uncle Jacob, Destiny's own father, shared any of it with her? With Aunt Fern? With his own brother? He had not inferred, one way or another, in his letter. Maybe I should let all of this go, be done with it, and quit searching. Nobody else seemed to be the least bit concerned.

I shared your email with Glory and River and they did not hesitate. They want to see you too. Neither of them are good with computers. Ben and I, and our kids, of course, have made it possible for them to stay secluded from the warp speed of life that swirls around us and we handle all their outside correspondence. Both our parents never wavered much from the trajectory they chose to pursue. Despite all the urbanization taking place within miles of the commune, they have managed to hold on to their last piece of paradise. You will see a lot of changes when you visit. Let me know when you will be arriving and I will share your response with them. Be well.

Des

It sounded cold, but to the point. I could hardly blame her for not becoming too enthusiastic, too quickly. She was, after all, the messenger. My response was mild and my heart raced as I read, and re-read, what I wrote. Hitting the "send" button was the worst invention of the computer age. Nothing, ever, was retrievable once that key was pressed.

Dear Destiny,

Thank you for getting back to me so quickly. You sound like you are a very busy mother, wife, and daughter. I am anxious to see everyone again, and I will let you know when the arrangements have been made. I will need to ask for time off work and let Andrew and the girls know of my plans as well. Please let Glory and River know I will see you all very soon.

Rose

It didn't get any more vanilla than that. At this point, I didn't want to offend anyone and didn't even sign my name with *Love*. Destiny hadn't. I followed her lead.

I SMELLED THE PEPPERMINT as soon as I opened the door to Betsy's office. She had cleared her desk of paperwork and mail to make room for the teacups and nodded in my direction. I was ready to discuss the offer I felt sure was imminent. I pushed all thoughts of Destiny, Uncle Jacob, River, Glory, all of them, to the back of my mind, in order to concentrate on the topic at hand. Her smile contradicted the conversation we were about to have.

"It's been a busy last couple of weeks, Rose." She sounded nonchalant at the start. "And I want you to know I've been pleased with the quality of your work and the success of the LA project. You were the right choice for this job."

Her demeanor shifted. As much as I wanted to respond, say thank you and acknowledge the praise she had bestowed on me, I remained silent while she continued.

"When you accepted this job, you mentioned you wanted to go back to a part-time position when the project was complete. I want you to know I respect your request, and it's why I have hired a new, full-time employee to move forward to the next phase of the company. I have no need for part-time designers. I'm really sorry, Rose, but I have already found your replacement. Actually, he's a past employee, and I reached out to him when I realized LA was coming to a close. We have to keep moving if we're going to continue to make a dent in the competition."

I could feel the blood rushing to my cheeks. I tried not to look offended. I was, after all, the one who was adamant six months ago that I didn't want to work full time. I sipped cautiously on the hot tea to give myself the seconds I needed to craft a response. "Do I know this person? A past employee?"

I realized in moments that she was not asking for a decision, the control I thought I had and conjured up in my head for days was non-existent. My role was to listen, accept, and leave. I managed a weak smile, and Betsy did the same.

"Yes, actually, you do. Remember Jack Chambers? I had to pry him away from his new job, sweeten the pot as it were, but he will need little training and the team worked well with him. I welcome his return."

I almost choked on the last swallow, and my eyes widened. I stopped myself from saying a word even though I seethed inside.

Betsy kept talking. "I know this probably comes as a surprise to you, Rose, but I know how much your family means to you. I will be happy to give you a stunning letter of recommendation if you ever want to pursue another part-time position with another firm. Anyone would be lucky to have you. I will need you to finish out the rest of this week, if you don't mind, in order to help close down the account and bring Jack up to speed. He will be stopping by the office on Friday."

My reaction was swift. I smiled to appear grateful that she was true to her promise to me. How could she know? All I wanted to do was make an excuse why I couldn't stay until Friday. No way did I want to encounter Jack, or be the one to 'bring him up to speed', as she'd suggested.

I did my best imitation of pleased. "Thank you for allowing me to assist with this project, Betsy. You've been a great boss, and I've learned a lot." I paused and took one more sip of tea. "But I don't think I can stay past Thursday. I've planned a trip to the Seattle area, and I leave Friday morning. I'm sure Jack will be able to pick up right where he left off."

CHAPTER 32

Andrew felt empathy for me, of course, but he also encouraged me to make the trip alone to see my parents. He had grown weary of my incessant probing, my need to pry into the private lives of my parents for too long, and he urged me to find some peace with myself and everyone else in the commune.

The girls were only mildly interested that I was leaving to see their grandparents, and they showed no desire to join me. I had created this pathetic mess, and it was up to me to repair it.

I loaded the front seat with my favorite CD's for the long trip and decided to stay overnight in a hotel once I crossed the Oregon border. I chose the first motel off the interstate that flashed a 'Vacancy' sign, relieved when I saw family vans and sedans parked in tandem with semi-trucks and trailers. No warning bells went off in my head even though I asked for the room closest to the lobby. A little extra assurance couldn't hurt.

Though not for lack of trying, I couldn't sleep. Thoughts raced through my mind, my well-rehearsed greeting to my parents kept shifting, and I almost made myself sick. No amount of tossing and turning stopped my imagination from running wild. I called Andrew far too late, but I needed to hear his soothing voice, much like I hungered for it when I had made this same trip that first summer after we started dating. He was still my anchor, and he never cut me loose no matter how rough I made our waters.

He knew what to say. "Hello, my love. Can't sleep?"

"Oh, Andrew, I'm so sorry to call so late, but you're right. I've been tossing and turning in my bed for the last two hours. Lots of noise on the interstate."

"That all that's keeping you awake? I'm having trouble, too. I don't want you to be worried, Rose. You're doing the right thing. You've made the right choice to visit your parents and repair the damage. That's all you need to know."

I imagined him propped up in bed where he had let the television lull him into a fitful slumber, one that I had interrupted. It was so Andrew to not be phased.

The tightness in my chest started to fade, and the longer we talked, the more relaxed I felt. We talked about our life, our girls, our choices, how lucky we were. My spirits lifted, because I knew at that moment that no matter what might happen with River and Glory, I would always have Andrew, Caroline, and Nicole to come home to.

"Okay, my love. Time for both of us to try this sleeping thing again. It's coming up on dawn. But one more thing before we hang up."

I was almost too tired now to be curious. "Yes?"

"I've been giving it a lot of thought. Get the damn DNA test. Find your truth once and for all. I will always be here for you, no matter what you find out."

I had not expected to hear this from him, ever, and I was speechless.

I WAS SATISFIED WITH FOUR HOURS sleep and pulled myself together the best I could before I grabbed breakfast in the community room and topped off the tank for the eight-hour drive to the commune. I selected my music with care, rock and roll, a little bit of country, and 'music from the 80's' for the first five CD's.

The six-CD record changer afforded me the luxury of pre-loading my music. Twice through for each would bring me close to the end of my long drive, and the sixth, a classical collection of waltzes by Johann Strauss would help me unwind before I took the last leg up the long driveway to River and Glory's home. I never considered myself an expert on the music scene, but the pastoral melody of waltzes and overtures soothed. I needed to feel as relaxed as possible for what was about to unfold.

Destiny said I would see a lot of changes since the last time I had been to the commune, my wedding day. I never thought so many years would separate me from one visit to the next. Instead of long stretches of open space in between communities, the streets and roads were overrun with fast food restaurants, gas stations, small developments tucked in between and that stretched to the east and west of the interstate.

The tranquil valleys of my memories had disappeared. The closer I got to River and Glory's, the more I prayed for the landscape to change back to the way it had once been - when the closest shopping center to the commune was ten miles away and there was a handful of stores that served the locals, including Goodwill. The high school Destiny and I attended was twenty miles out of town, the junior high a bit farther down the road. What was once country reserved for outliers, fringe refugees from the city, young idealists from my parent's generation, now looked like anywhere USA. Young families flocked, new businesses had sprung up, houses were constructed almost overnight, freeway exits multiplied and parks and playgrounds occupied the countryside in abundance. It felt crowded and painful as I made my way closer to what had once been my home.

I remembered the turn-off, the steep driveway, the gravel road that led to the house. My sense of direction played tricks on me. I couldn't figure out where I was, or if I had overshot my turn. The once open natural fields at the bottom of our hill had been replaced with two large pillars built higher than any structure inside the neighborhood. It was an engineering masterpiece, created with artistic genius, modern flair, and money. Andrew would be impressed.

The curved construction consisted of a river rock embellishment at the base of the post, with stones of assorted sizes that carried the color palette of blacks and ivory. A splash of gray and tan mixed in attempted to create the illusion that it had been a long-standing piece of the landscape, not something erected in record time with artificial materials. It could be seen from a mile away, and in four-foot tall brass letters the words Harmony Acres spanned across the opening.

Are you kidding me? Is this supposed to be a play on the idea that the developers had purchased the land from some hippies? Some kind of peace movement or something? A way to attract buyers with a name that sounded safe, warm, harmless? None of the new citizens would ever know what it was like to encounter true calm and tranquility.

I pulled over to the well-manicured side of the road, now resplendent with sidewalks, streetlights, flowering shrubs, and a perfect row of emerald green arborvitae that gave the illusion of an upscale neighborhood. The place where any college-educated, well-paid, young executive would want to raise a family. Once past the entrance, I looked beyond the cul-de-sacs on either side, and I took the only road that looked familiar up a private drive. I turned off the music, perfectly timed with the last lilting note of The Blue Danube. I could hear the stream. *They kept the stream. They negotiated the stream.* I pressed my hand to my heart and smiled.

AS IF PASSING THROUGH a magic window of time, the two-lane entrance narrowed down to a single, country road and exposed an isolated grove of fruit trees and strawberry fields. I rolled down the window, inhaling the familiar aroma of citrus and apple blossoms. Sounds I remembered as a child, dogs barking, children shouting back and forth, Destiny's voice in the background, "Seth, get your brother and sister, come inside, and wash up for dinner. We're expecting company. I don't want you to look like orphans when she gets here."

She hadn't seen me as I slowly maneuvered up the hill and approached the house within earshot of her voice. *She must be talking about me. I'm sure she is. I haven't heard that voice in so long.*

I saw Glory and River reach for each of Destiny's children with a quick embrace as they marched through the door. Seth was about fourteen, Caroline and her second boy were born not too far apart, so he would be about twelve. My Nicole and Des's little girl were close in age.

Glory looked thin and River looked exactly the same. A little more gray, but still a full head of hair and the mustache that wasn't going anywhere.

I forced myself to breathe in slow even measures as I pulled the car into an open space closest to the house. I checked myself in the rear view mirror as if there was anything I would be able to do at that time if my mascara was running or my lipstick was smeared. I couldn't wait one more second. My approach signaled a greeting from three large dogs in unison. I was surrounded by the animals within seconds. River bounded down the stairs to greet me and make some order out of the chaos. Glory steadied herself on the railing and waved, a smile so pure and utterly devoid of anger or hate.

I had never forgotten that smile, and I felt warmed and loved by it at that moment. Destiny stood behind her three children. The aroma that drifted from inside the house was unmistakable...*Glory's buttermilk biscuits.* It was like I had never left. The chasm had already begun to disappear.

CHAPTER 33

I noticed that Glory clung to the railing as she waited for me to join her. Destiny moved her brood to one side, allowing my mother to greet me with open arms. She held on as if for dear life and her frailty belied her physical strength. I stood at least six inches above her. I was careful not to squeeze too hard, but her embrace felt hearty and strong. She felt thin in my arms, but her eyes sparkled when she stepped back and exclaimed, "Rose, my beautiful Rose. All of a sudden it doesn't feel like it has been almost ten years. It feels like it was yesterday, and you are as beautiful as ever."

I saw Destiny wipe her eye, maybe a tear?

The greetings erupted. River took my mother by the hand as if to remove her from the commotion so she would not fall. No one had told me Glory had been ill. I prayed that she was not, even though it was hard not to notice the change in her.

Maybe she's getting over the flu. That would knock anyone down, especially someone as delicate as Glory.

The fuss around me settled, I was introduced to Destiny's children, and felt deeply grateful for her affectionate embrace. I looked past everyone, noticing Aunt Fern and Uncle Jacob as they walked towards me, dish towels in hand. Both extended their arms and welcomed me at the same time with an enveloping hug.

"We're just waiting for Ben to get back with tonight's pickings from the garden," Aunt Fern offered. "He didn't want any of us to miss your arrival, said he would catch up with all of us at the dinner table."

"And that smell....that one-of-a-kind, Glory made buttermilk biscuits, hot out of the oven, smell." I rolled my eyes with pure joy and every negative thought I had carried for a decade drifted away. My only regret was that Andrew, Caroline, and Nicole were not with me to share this memory. I had no doubt there would be more, but this particular moment in time was mine to savor.

"SHE HARDLY ATE A THING." I opened the conversation with Destiny as we walked the familiar path together towards the stream, alone, after dinner. "Is there something I should know?"

"There's so much you don't know about your mother, about us, what twists and turns our lives have taken since you've been away."

I didn't remind her that it was her, not me, who cut off communication. That I had reached out more than once through letters and emails to all of them. They might as well have sent a group text that said, "Hey, Rose, just so you know, you're cut off." Destiny had no idea of my struggles or what I had gone through without any of them in my life, and even if I had been the genesis, I was as profoundly affected as they were. I didn't say a word, though.

She stepped over a large boulder and kept her head down,

eyes trained on the winding path. We had dodged the hazard of snakes, lizards, scorpions and other creatures on the trail that led us to what we thought was the most perfect spot on earth when we were children. I lifted my head high enough to see the grove of trees in the distance, and I marveled at how it was exactly as my memory served.

It was hard to believe that beyond it were five hundred homes, a movie theatre, mega warehouse shopping centers, home improvements stores, gas stations, schools, parks. My parents, Uncle Jacob and Aunt Fern had driven a hard bargain in order to preserve their rightful spot, and they had managed to keep their bubble a secret from the world that roared by them every day.

"There, the big boulder under the tree." I pointed in the direction of the perfect location to stop. No need. Destiny already led the way.

"You look good, Rose. I didn't know how I would react when I saw you. I've been angry at you for a long time."

I was prepared to take my licks. "Don't blame you. I've been angry at me a long time, too." My last comment brought a chuckle from both of us. "How long has Glory been sick?"

"I don't know if it's my place to tell you anything, Rose. I think you need to talk with her and River yourself. She's not been well for the last year. She's just finished another round of tests. I'm not sure of the results. Not my place. Jacob and Fern spend a lot of time over there helping out."

I stared straight ahead, studied every ripple in the stream, how it gently rolled over a rock in some places or slapped against the shore in others. I noticed little gnats that hovered just above the surface, while small birds balanced themselves amongst the branches that dipped into the water with a strong breeze. Life was abundant, and it was beautiful.

Please don't tell me that Glory is going to die.

"One question, Des, then I'll be quiet and we can talk about something else." My eyes fixated on the sun's rays casting streaks of light on the water - brilliant, glistening, and inordinately beautiful compared to the conversation at hand. I could barely say the word. It was ugly to hear and left a sharp, unpleasant taste in my mouth that lingered long after it was uttered. "Cancer?"

Destiny nodded.

EVERYTHING I THOUGHT would happen on my trip, didn't. I didn't approach Uncle Jacob about his revelation, I didn't question River about my paternity. I didn't tell any of them I dropped the DNA test off at a lab the day before I left the Bay Area. I didn't do anything to press anyone into an admission or offer further explanation of a life they lived when they were not much older than Caroline and Seth.

I checked in with the girls and Andrew every evening, and he commented more than once on how relaxed I sounded. "Fresh air has a way of doing that to a body," I said. "And it's been wonderful. I'll tell you more when I get home. Kiss the girls...tell them I miss them and love them very much and next time, we all visit together."

"They would like that." Andrew sounded convincing, then changed the subject. "Have you talked to Jacob about the letter? About the possibility of getting a DNA test?"

I was glad for Andrew's support. I hadn't mentioned anything to him either. He didn't know I had already left the sample with the lab, one strand of hair from Uncle Jacob and a cheek swab taken by a lab assistant from me. Four to six weeks, they said. I still had time to decide what, if anything, I would do with the results. I felt purged of the echoes of the past, and I wanted to spend my last two days with Glory and River free of accusations and pain. "Nah. Not yet. We can talk later."

THE NEXT MORNING, the opportunity presented itself when I noticed Glory on the front porch by herself, cloaked in a pink, fuzzy bathrobe that draped around her tiny frame. All I could see were the strands of her bangs, the shawl collar pulled tight around her neck, and her big, blue eyes studying the rising sun. Her hands were wrapped around a familiar mug, bright colored daisies on the outside, yellow on the inside, and wisps of steam escaping into the cold morning air.

It was early. I had hoped to steal a cup of coffee by myself before River came downstairs. I didn't expect Glory to be awake. Her voice broke the silence. "I made an extra big pot of coffee. Mug is on the counter. Had to ask your father to climb a ladder so he could bring it down from the top shelf." I knew the mug before I saw it.

"It's still in one piece, amazing for a fifty-cent mug," I said from the kitchen. My matching cup, except for the orange color on the inside, waited for me by the fresh pot of coffee. I was glad she hadn't thrown it away. I grabbed a blanket from the back of the couch and joined her.

"Something I need to tell you, Rose."

I sat with her, opened the blanket to full size, and gently placed it over both our laps. She seemed so tiny and fragile. "I know," I muttered under my breath. "Good coffee, Glory. A really good pot." I wanted to stall the inevitable. I couldn't.

"I'm sure you've noticed that something is different about me. I'm not quite as healthy as you remember. Of course, you do. You never missed anything."

I thought I saw a slight upward turn of her lips as she conjured up the thought of my inquisitive nature.

It hurt to look at her, and I felt helpless as she tried to find a comfortable position under the cover that obscured her delicate body from view. Glory didn't look at me, nor I her. We both stared straight ahead at the rising sun, moments away from a gradual emergence of light that would signify the start of a new day. She never mentioned the 'C' word. She didn't have to. I knew enough to string together the meaning of CT scan, hysterectomy, chemotherapy, and another dreaded word, almost worse than 'cancer'…metastasized.

"No more treatment."

I could barely hear her.

She took slow, deliberate sips of the hot brew, drawing deep breaths every now and then in an effort to expand her lungs and provide her with the strength that she needed to speak.

My head was an explosion of sound, screaming from the inside, silenced by my desire to not create a moment that was worse than the news I had just received. We cried together softly, our free hands wrapped together, our mugs now half-full of lukewarm coffee, and we watched a new day begin.

Glory turned to me and smiled. "We have today. I'm glad you're here, Rose."

I started to let her know how sorry I was, about her illness, about the years that were wasted by my hurtful comments, but she stilled me. I could see she wanted to have the final words to this difficult conversation. It was like she had practiced what she would say for a very long time.

"Jacob told me about the letter he sent you, and we both agreed you must do whatever is necessary to bring you peace. We all did our best, dear Rose."

"Did he tell you he shared that Andrew was adopted?" I wasn't sure if Uncle Jacob had made this overture to reach out to me on his own or if Glory had urged him to follow through.

"Yes. That was kind of Jacob to lead the way. We didn't know how to tell you what you had long suspected, regardless of what you find out, but to have you continue to think that Andrew was your cousin was too much to bear. We didn't want this to come between you and your husband, or ruin another generation with doubts, questions...lies. I hope you understand why this was the most important message in his letter."

I tried to respond, and once again was hushed with a slight touch of her hand on mine.

"Let me finish. You don't need to say anything." She lowered her eyes, gathering her courage to impart final words of wisdom. She raised her head, looked straight into my eyes, now welling with tears. "The fault is mine. I was unprepared to hear what you had to say, felt accused of something that was so shameful, and it immediately put me on the defensive. I was guilty...my secret was so deep, I thought if I kept it to myself, it would simply erase the mistake...like it never happened. I don't know the answer any more than Jacob does. We were both hoping it would never be brought up again, but always afraid it would. A stupid mistake of foolish teenagers, unrepentant until the reality of my pregnancy was confirmed. I'm sorry, Rose. I don't know what else to say except I have always loved you. I have always loved River. You are my world and I helped bring it crashing down. I'm so sorry."

Her thin body started to quiver. I didn't know if she was cold or the subject matter was overwhelming her senses. I helped her pull the cover tighter, leaving only her hands and her face exposed. "One more thing. I have to tell you one last thing so you don't think I was a horrible child for creating a distance between my parents and myself."

Stop, Glory, please stop. You don't have to torture yourself.

"You must have thought I was a terrible person, a selfish daughter, and an uncaring mother, to keep you from your grandmother all those years."

Whatever I had thought in the past instantly evaporated. She was talking about me, too. The similarities were not lost on me. "No, Glory! Please don't talk like that. You have never been uncaring or selfish to me, or River, or anyone!"

I reeled in every bad thought I had ever harbored towards my parents and felt they might physically purge themselves from my body. I felt nauseous, like I might throw up. I was terrified for Glory, in her weakened state, bearing such a heavy load.

"I have to tell you one more thing, Rose."

"Only if you want to, Glory. I didn't come here to see you dredge up painful memories. That's not why I'm here." I pleaded, "I just wanted to *see* you. See River, Destiny, Uncle Jacob, Aunt Fern...everyone." I must have sounded lost, deflated. No words would ever undo the damage we all had suffered for almost a decade.

She squeezed my hand harder, a herculean effort on her part. Glory's strength had been sapped to the point that this one simple gesture was barely noticeable. "You should know this. It's time." I did my best to stay calm.

"When I got pregnant, I was barely eighteen years old, just out of high school, with dreams of college, a career, a family one day. I hadn't quite made up my mind what I wanted to be, but I had already been accepted to San Francisco State and my parents were elated. When my father, who was hardly ever around, found out, he was horrified and said I had one choice if I intended to continue living under their roof." She squeezed her eyes shut as if the memory of that moment was still as painful as the day she lived through it.

I held my breath. I sensed what she would say next.

"He said I would have to get an abortion. It was barely legal. Young girls were still visiting dirty clinics in dark alleys to get butchered by unlicensed providers or worse yet, terminating their own pregnancies with a coat hanger, many of them not surviving their own cruel hand. This is what my father wanted for his daughter." She started to cry, softly, not sobs, but a silent release of a memory tinged with such enormous pain, it changed the whole trajectory of her life.

I wanted to lessen her pain. It was more than I could bear to see, watching this burden creep back into her life, a heartache that had been hidden for years. *She wasn't much older than Caroline, for Christ's sake.*

She continued, her voice cracking with emotion. "There was no way I was going to get an abortion, and the thought of letting go of a life I had helped to create was out of the question." She opened her eyes and turned to me. Our eyes locked. "I could never have given you up, Rose. Whoever that little person was growing inside me was my child. And it was you, Rose, my beautiful baby girl."

My mind raced. I questioned whether or not to continue the conversation, but Glory could not be stopped. With every ounce of strength she had, she intended to finish.

"My mother sided with my father. I learned later that she only did so because she was afraid that if she objected, if she had protected me instead of obeying him, he would divorce her and leave her penniless. She had never worked, couldn't support herself, was so emotionally drained from the loss of their first born and lack of affection from my father, she shielded herself from more loss."

"But she took such good care of me, you know she did."

"Yes, I know. We made our peace years ago, Rose, at your wedding."

So that's what all those midnight talks over ice cream were all about. I always wondered what kept you both up so late.

I got it, all of it. My mother's words stayed with me long after that conversation.

"All I ask now is please, please, please don't blame any of us, including yourself, for being human."

We sat in silence until the house rustled with River's awakening and the aroma of the second pot of freshly-brewed coffee drifted in our direction. My mother's eyes lit up. "Good morning, River. Come join us." She made a gesture to the worn Adirondack chair, slightly damp from the morning dew. I jumped up, rushed past River into the kitchen and dashed back outside with a dry towel. I could see a big grin on his face as he ambled onto the porch, pushed the chair next to Glory, and nestled himself into the seat.

"Yes, it is...a very good morning," he said before taking a sip of the steaming brew and reaching out for Glory's hand.

"I'LL BE BACK SOON. Next time, with Andrew and the girls. They will love it here," I gushed. But it was the truth. Caroline could see her Papa that she barely remembered, and Nicole would light up their lives with her constant chatter and never-ending questions.

I looked first at River, then holding back the tears, to Glory as they escorted me to my car. My mother navigated the unsteady path and clutched River's and my hands for support. The pack of dogs, once barking and uncontrollable, were calm and serene. They ambled alongside us, as though the guardians of our fate. I felt torn at that moment. I didn't want to leave. I couldn't wait to return.

CHAPTER 34

Although I was impatient to share the news with Andrew and anxious to hear the sound of his voice that would make it all better, I decided to wait until I got home. I took an extra day driving back and hoped to wring out one last morsel of serenity before rejoining the hectic pace of the city and the demands of a lifestyle that had once been my dream. Andrew assured me he didn't mind. He had everything under control.

When I pulled into the driveway, it was almost 10 o'clock at night. The porch light illuminated the path to the front door. I could see the glow in the family room from the lamp on the end table, and Andrew's silhouette in a reclining position with an open book on his chest.

My guy, waiting up for me.

I didn't want to startle him. He stirred when he heard my key in the door. He was wide awake by the time I set down my suitcase in the entryway, and he stood to greet me. He caught me off guard when he met me with an all-enveloping hug without saying a word.

His arms tightened around my shoulders when I asked, "What's wrong? Something's wrong. I can tell."

I pushed back slightly from his embrace, but he refused to

let go. He strengthened his grip around my shoulders and drew me closer. I could tell something was bothering him. He looked like he may have been crying. It would have to be something really terrible for Andrew to cry.

He tried to lead me to the couch. "Let's go into the family room and sit down, Rose."

I resisted his tug and looked up at him again.

"No, Andrew, what's wrong? Tell me right here. I'm not moving." My thoughts immediately raced to Glory. I froze when I thought it could be Caroline or Nicole. Had something happened to one of them? "Where are the girls?"

"Fine, they're fine." He reached for my hand.

I held tight to stay upright. I knew then, but had to ask. "Glory?"

My legs felt like they would give way beneath me. Andrew steadied me. I didn't have to ask again, a slow nod, and a look on his face so sorrowful, we both burst into tears. We stood in the dark for what felt like an eternity.

In between uncontrollable sobs, I managed to ask, "When? How long? I just left them....I didn't think it would be this soon! It's not fair!"

"A few hours ago. River called and said he didn't want to call you while you were driving. He didn't want you to be alone when you got the news. What happened, Rose? Why didn't you tell me Glory was sick?"

I took a deep breath to halt the tears, wiping them with the back of my hand. I whimpered, "I was going to tell you everything when I got home. I didn't want to talk about it on the phone." I started to cry again. "I didn't know it was this bad. No one told me how bad it was and that she was going to die so soon!"

"Maybe they didn't know. I'm sure River and Glory

would have told you if they did." Andrew put one hand on each shoulder and held me at arm's length. His eyes were red and swollen. "Rose, promise me one thing." He didn't wait for me to say 'ok', 'yes', 'no', 'maybe'. He wasn't waiting for an answer. "Promise me you will concentrate on this last, wonderful week with your mother and father and not dwell on the real or imagined slights that led you down this path. Your parents have always loved you, and you have always loved them. Let it go."

I nodded and whispered, "Okay."

RIVER AND I TALKED EVERY DAY. He was beside himself. I offered to come back to help with Glory's memorial, put off for a month to contact old friends and commune members who had once shared their dream. He told me he didn't see any reason for me to make the trip again and there wasn't anything I could do. Destiny, Fern, and Jacob were there to help. As much as he wanted to see me again, along with the girls and Andrew, he asked for a little more time.

"I don't want you to see me like this, Rose. Maybe by next month I'll be feeling more like my old self. Besides, Glory often said she wanted to be buried in the same cemetery as her parents, hoping she could accomplish something in death that she could never do in life. I'm still not sure where the memorial will be...maybe in San Francisco. I'm still thinking about it."

Almost forty years of marriage and never one night apart. I couldn't fathom the depth of his loss. I waited for him to come to me. I wondered if Glory or Uncle Jacob told him about the letter, but had no desire to ask. I was beginning to understand the dream my parents chased, to work towards the common good instead of living a self-serving existence. It was great in theory, but difficult in reality.

Still, River, Glory, Uncle Jacob, and Aunt Fern managed to keep their vision alive. It was starting to look much more attractive to me than the daily grind of the city and the disconnected life I had created for myself.

ANDREW LOOKED HAGGARD when he came home from work that night. He'd spent a lot of time in front of the television lately, watching CNN for hours, and our conversations often shifted to the stock market and recession. Some areas of the country had already started to crumble beneath the weight of the plunging Dow, and the real estate market was starting to falter.

Building had come to a screeching halt. Developers were filing for bankruptcy left and right. Liar loans and unscrupulous lending practices had made it easy for anyone to buy a brand new home, without stating their income. Home builders and banks, once working in concert to sell to any gullible buyer, were now shuttering their doors and offering little or no help to alleviate the financial stress on the American public.

The Bay Area held its own, but the pinch was starting to trickle down. Even the wealthiest were affected. Baby boomers saw their life saving's cut in half while they slept. Banks started to foreclose on middle class families who had been convinced they could afford the home of their desires, even when their salaries couldn't support the mortgage payment.

Developments no more than two years old had a glut of

for sale signs up and down the streets of once manicured, model-ready homes. As home values plummeted, investors, waving cash offers at the banks and sellers who hoped to be released from their suffocating debt, created a flurry of multiple bids and whole blocks were turned into a surplus of rentals.

The American dream was turning into a nightmare, and Andrew had every reason to be concerned. It was 2008, my mother had just died. I braced myself for more bad news.

WE NEVER TALKED FINANCES in front of our girls. Growing up in a fast-paced environment, social networks using kids as punching bags, bad news reaching one end of the world to another in a matter of seconds, left little time for them to be children. Neither Andrew nor I could relate to the stresses of pre-adolescence like Caroline and Nicole had become accustomed, and we did our best to keep somber conversations private.

"This is getting serious, isn't it?" I asked as I joined him in the family room.

Andrew didn't look up, but turned down the volume on the television so we could talk. "It's not good, Rose. There's something I've been wanting to discuss with you, but with all the turmoil these past few weeks, I couldn't bear to add any more problems to the pile."

"I'm not sure you could tell me anything worse than what's already happened, and whatever it is, we're a team. We'll get through." Although no genius when it came to finances, I was well aware of the impact on families like ours and what the recession could mean to our future. "Does this have something to do with work?"

"How did you know?"

"I might not be glued to the news channels all night like you, but I do read the paper. The hardest part is admitting that we're all in trouble, this recession is really happening, the Bernie Madoff's of the world are being indicted for perpetrating these financial crimes on our country, but that is little consolation to the tens of thousands of people out of a job. Regular working class dads are jumping off bridges and killing their families. It feels like the whole country is distraught, and I try my best to NOT think about it." I came to the end of my sentence, breathless. The ramifications were too harsh to consider. "I wonder how this will affect River...." I let my part of the conversation drift off to nothingness.

"River and the rest of them will probably be affected far less. They already know how to live off the land, and they've managed for decades without the intervention of credit cards or checking accounts. I'm sure they will be fine. We, on the other hand, might not be. I don't want to worry you just yet, but ..."

"You already have," I interrupted. "Can you tell me what's going on, please? With you, with us?"

"My boss has prepared all the partners for a re-organization. Two out of the five of us will be let go, but he hasn't named anyone yet. We all have families, no one deserves to stay or go more than the others. Someone is just going to get the short end of the stick. It's the only way the firm will be able to ride out the recession. Business has dropped steadily for the last six months, and this last month was the worst one yet."

Andrew trained his eyes on the TV, not me, even though there was no volume and the same news was repeated over and over. It never sounded more hopeful, simply a reiteration of the calamity as it unfolded twenty-four hours a day.

I wondered if Betsy faced the same problem. Would I be able to find another job? Would Andrew be able to make a good enough living to continue to support us, and would there be any jobs available in his field if he was asked to leave? I stared at the pictures on the screen as well, the two of us absorbing the tickertape headlines below the newscaster, which silently revealed more bad news.

The phone interrupted our soundless vigil. It was River. I grabbed it. "Have to get this," I mouthed to Andrew. He flashed a thumbs up without averting his gaze from the set.

I looked forward to River's phone calls and it had been a couple days since I'd last heard from him. His voice sounded stronger. "Rose, wanted to let you know the memorial has been planned for next week, in San Francisco as Glory wanted. Most of our old friends migrated back to the area, a few in Southern California. Everyone we've contacted so far said they wanted to attend. I'll call you tomorrow with the details."

I was relieved we wouldn't have to make the trip. Caroline and Nicole had shown concern for me, but it was obvious they couldn't relate to my pain. They barely knew who Glory and River were and Nicole had only seen them in pictures. Caroline had only shared one Christmas with them. A distant memory, if she remembered any of it.

CHAPTER 35

I had become practiced at pushing thoughts aside, especially since there was not much to think about lately that made me smile. I'd forgotten about the DNA test I had dropped off six weeks earlier and was not prepared when it arrived. How I could let that thought slip my mind was a mystery to me, but somehow, it had fallen to the bottom of my list of priorities.

It peeked out from the stack of mail, in between grocery store ads and four more pieces of marketing material from scam lenders and banks no one had ever heard of, promising a quick fix to the financial woes of those in peril of foreclosure or eviction. The same disreputable businesses that had gotten us here in the first place still preyed upon and counted on the gullibility of the masses. I set the bills to one side, retrieved the envelope from the lab, and tucked it under one arm.

My day of reckoning had arrived. My imagination would support my fears or alter the course of my life forever. I stalled, took my time to walk outside to the back of the garage and added the circulars and junk mail to the recycle bin. The four-ounce bulk of the legal-sized envelope under my arm felt like it weighed a ton. The ramifications of its contents contained a much heavier burden. I seated myself in the

Herman Miller luxurious and expensive office chair that had been a splurge. It promised to keep us cool and dry, regardless of the season, reduce back and neck pain from long hours at the desk, a forward tilt to prevent slouching and improve our comfort.

I'm sure a less expensive version from a discount store would have served the same purpose. I wondered how Glory and River might have reacted if they had known we spent on a chair what they did on three months' worth of groceries.

I laid the envelope on the desk and rocked back and forth on the well-grounded, rubber casters of our expensive piece of furniture. I pulled the letter opener from the caddy on the desk, a jumble of pens, highlighters, and mechanical pencils. Poised with it in my right hand, I turned over the letter and pushed the needle-sharp instrument into the small hole not affected by the glue on the envelope flap...one small gap, barely large enough to allow the penetration of the pointed end of the tool. I heard the smooth tear of paper, the whoosh of one deft motion. I peered inside in hopes I would see a revelation without the need to unfold the letter.

I fumbled for the edge of the tri-fold message and drew a deep breath before I opened it. I stopped myself short of reading past the salutation, *Dear Rose.* I read it again. *Dear Rose.*

Two words spoke volumes. It was at that moment I realized it made no difference what the rest of the letter would reveal. Nothing would or could ever change the fact that I am Rose. No DNA test or question of paternity would make a difference. I am that person, named Rose, who by any other name would still be me no matter the identity of my father, where I was raised, the color my eyes, or how tall I had grown.

My hands started to sweat. I withdrew the 4-page

document, complete with explanations of the test results, most of which were unimportant. I searched the first page for definitive proof, but it was filled with descriptions of the process, scientific explanation of the tests, and legal disclaimers that I glossed over.

I pressed on and forced myself to turn to the last page, the one with the answer I had been searching for my entire life. And there it was, in black and white. A conclusive statement in bold print that this test was 99.9% accurate. I knew. I finally knew. Uncle Jacob's and my DNA samples were a match.

I rolled the chair over to the corner of the office, turned the switch of the shredder to the on position, and smiled as I watched the letter turn into narrow ribbons of information that no longer mattered.

CHAPTER 36

I gazed around the room, craned my neck with every new person who entered, and wondered if I would recognize anyone after all these years. Andrew grabbed my arm as if to steady me, even though I didn't need his assistance. What I did need was to concentrate on the ceremony, but too many unanswered questions swirled around us and life-changing decisions needed to be made. We were still waiting for the final announcement from his company that would either make or break us, determine whether or not we could afford to remain in the city, or if we would need to start looking for an apartment, pull the girls from their private school, and start all over.

"Leave your cell phones at home today," I instructed Caroline and Nicole before we left the house.

Dual groans of disappointment flooded the air. "I don't want to go to a funeral today. I had other plans. I didn't even know her. Can't I stay home?" Caroline tried her best to squirm out of the obligation, but Andrew extended his hands to both daughters and confiscated the instruments.

"You could have at least warned us. None of my friends will know where I am today. How am I going to keep up? It will be dark before we get home. Does this mean I can't go to the slumber party tonight?" Caroline's sulky nature was in full force and she had no problem making her feelings known.

"Don't waste your breath," I overheard Andrew whisper in our eldest daughter's ear. "It won't do you any good."

He was quiet and calm as usual, but I caught the expression on his face and the stern look he conveyed in order to bring Caroline's boil to a low simmer.

We took our seats as the service was ready to begin, in the front row, with family. The girls were fidgety and restless and clearly didn't want to be there. Their fingers twitched on invisible cell phones and it was not hard to tell they weren't mentally in the moment. They had not been a part of their mother's family and history, and I had no one to blame but myself.

"Please settle down, girls," I hushed them. "Try to act more like the age you are instead of petulant toddlers. This is important to me."

As the final mourners streamed in and the room began to quiet, I leaned over and whispered to Andrew, "The letter from the lab came last week." I didn't allow him to respond and rushed to finish my thought. "I shredded it."

He laid his hand on my knee and acknowledged my comment with a familiar, supportive squeeze. He whispered his response, "My curious Rose. I never would have thought you would shred the results without looking."

He jumped to this conclusion, and I didn't correct him. "It's too bad you wasted so many precious years chasing this thing. This stupid thing you thought was so important. I love you, Rose. I hope today will bring you some peace."

He was right. I had chased this 'thing' into the ground. Today would be the end of it, or the beginning. I felt both anxious and scared. I saw River talking with the minister, head down, trying not to cry. River, Aunt Fern, Uncle Jacob - they were now three instead of four, and they all looked hollow and desolate.

I pictured walking up to my father after the service, without the slightest idea of what might happen. I was prepared for anything. I just didn't know what.

ANDREW GRIPPED MY HAND during the eulogy. It was Uncle Jacob who spoke. River could barely string two sentences together and my heart broke into a million pieces as I watched him struggle to control his emotions. I clutched Andrew's arm and buried my head in his shoulder, secure that he would never leave me. I didn't even want to tell him I was right. That yes, I may have chased this 'thing' my entire life, but I had good reason to question and I finally knew the truth.

It was not all my fault that River and Glory harbored this secret from me their entire lives. All I craved at that moment was peace. I knew I would never see my mother again, hear her voice or touch her hand, but I felt her presence all around. It was as if she was right there with me, murmuring softly, "You will do the right thing, Rose. I know you will do the right thing."

"And so, for those of you who have come to say goodbye to Caroline Nicole ..." Both my daughters took notice and cast a quizzical look in my direction. "...let us remember that she will always be a part of us and her gift of love will never fade. Be thankful that you were touched by her light and can continue to share her message of harmony and forgiveness by the words you use, the thoughts you ponder and the actions you pursue. Be kind and take care of one another, always."

The minister closed his prayer book and took a few steps back. River got up from his front row seat and walked with slow, restrained steps, unsure if he could take the last one, knowing that once he did so, he would never be in Glory's presence again.

I released my grip on Andrew and watched the procession of old friends join River, Aunt Fern and Uncle Jacob. I wanted to wait until everyone had filed past, paid their last respects, until I joined the trio. I needed to make this moment count, not only for me, but for my father. Andrew and the girls stayed behind in their seats, their eyes trained on me as I approached my mother's casket. I glanced at Uncle Jacob and nodded. And there stood my father, waiting for my embrace, an open invitation.

I stared up at River and drank in the warmth of his deep blue eyes. As he enveloped me with his aging, but muscular arms, I felt the connection of father and daughter, thwarted only by my own stubbornness, my own insistence of learning the truth. I could physically feel River's pain of his enormous loss.

My mother's death was unforgiving, the toll on him only beginning to be taken, yet amidst his sorrow, he found a way to forgive me for the missing years, the unmade memories and the pain I had visited upon him and Glory.

I turned my head to one side, and caught a glimpse of Uncle Jacob as he supported Aunt Fern. She fumbled in her purse for a tissue, her tear-streaked face etched in grief, unaware of the fleeting eye contact between us. Without sound, I mouthed, "Thank you."

His wordless response was instantaneous as I detected a broad smile, along with an affirmative nod of his head. It was not important that Uncle Jacob know the answer. He could read into it whatever he wanted. My heart was at peace.

River released his grip on me. I motioned to Caroline and Nicole. "Girls, come on over. Say hello to your grandfather."

CHAPTER 37

"Two of you will be let go?" Andrew and I continued to wonder what would become of our home and our family if one of them was him.

"Next week. My boss said they would send out a memo and for all of us to be prepared."

"It sounds like doomsday. What if you decided to quit? Then only one of you would be affected."

Andrew said that I must be crazy, why would he take a chance like that? What if he wasn't one of the partners on the chopping block? "Do you know something I don't know?"

It was a serious topic, but I felt lighthearted. "I wouldn't have brought it up if I didn't have an option. Heard from River this morning."

"I hope he isn't asking us to come up for a visit just yet. We have too many other things on our plate right now."

"Sit down, my handsome guy." I really was in a playful mood. I led him to the couch and stood over him, not ready to take a seat beside him. "What if....." I faltered and started again. "What if we sold the house, got out from under our mortgage, and moved in with River? The house is big enough, now that it has been remodeled, and the girls will each have their own room."

"You sound excited. Like you've already thought this through."

The conversation had hit a speed bump and he looked like he was deep in thought. "I assume River asked us to move in with him?" I nodded an enthusiastic yes. "And you, my Rose, after running away from your humble beginnings are now eager to return?" I added another enthusiastic yes.

He scratched his head and looked confused. He had every right. "What would I do with myself all day? What would you do? How do we break this to the girls?"

"Every right to be concerned. I haven't had time to figure all of that out, but River and Uncle Jacob are getting much older and Ben can hardly keep up with the orchards on his own." Andrew lifted his eyes to meet mine.

"Oh...so now I'm going to be a farmer." He snapped his fingers and said in a sarcastic tone, "I knew I went to college for seven years for something! Gosh, Rose, I'd be thrilled to pick apples all day and sell produce every weekend at the corner store. My dream come true."

I was defeated, but not done. "I'm only trying to think of a way to survive this recession and make the best choice for all of us. The girls might not understand at first, but they can leave in a few years, just like I did. It doesn't have to be forever. I'm the last person to have ever thought moving *back* to the commune would be an answer, much less one that sounded like a perfect solution to what we might be facing."

With a resigned slump of his shoulders, Andrew shot back, "Can we at least wait until next week? Maybe my position will be spared and the rest of this conversation won't be necessary. Deal?"

"Deal."

IT WASN'T EASY TO CONVINCE Caroline and Nicole that we had to sell the house and would be moving to the commune for a short time. Neither Andrew nor I shared our real fears with the girls, but the outlook was grim for our immediate future.

Andrew and I were one of few who had the opportunity for a soft landing. Other homes in our community had already been put on the market and some of our neighbors chose to simply walk away. We had no other choice but to consider and accept River's offer.

I was delighted. Andrew resigned himself to the reality.

I tried to soften the blow for him, suggested he open a consulting business for a few years, until business picked up again. Negative at first, he thought it might be a consideration, but as our options dwindled, he warmed to the idea of working with his hands in the orchards, something he had abandoned when he left his parent's home for the city.

Both girls whined and complained in the back seat for most of the twelve-hour drive. Overnight, Andrew and I had been forced to make decisions that were unpleasant and gut-wrenching. We sold belongings that would bring in the most cash, like our second car, a brand new Volvo, built to last a lifetime. We opted to keep, much to the dismay of our daughters, our five-year-old SUV, still without dents or paint damage, but registering over 75,000 miles. It was paid for. No contest.

The dip in housing value was dramatic, especially in the outlying areas of the Bay Area. If you weren't in the middle of the city, close to tourism and large corporations, homes dipped precariously below their original purchase prices. The newer the home and homeowner, the more at-risk you were for losing it to the bank or an investor. Like vultures, they had prepared for a downturn market, stashed cash for their opportunity to acquire massive amounts of property, held them until the situation stabilized, then doubled their investment in record time. We got lucky. The profit we had made over the years vanished overnight, but we were able to salvage our original down payment, enough for a few years and plenty to ensure our survival.

ANDREW AND I DID OUR BEST to make the slow trip to River's as pleasant as possible. We stopped paying attention to the mumbling and grumbling behind our backs. The girls were almost teenagers, accustomed to the newest gadgets, nicest clothes, and hours of browsing and spending money at the mall, with no idea of how it was earned or how hard their parents had to work for it.

For all of River's and Glory's examples - buy only what you need, live within your means, share what you have, put the needs of others before yourself, value people above self, care about the welfare of the group - it had been lost on me...until now.

Caroline broke into my thoughts. "I hate this place. I'm leaving as soon as I turn eighteen!"

Andrew and I turned to one another, and slight smiles crept across our faces. "Sound familiar, my love?"

"Very," I said. I turned my head around and faced our daughters. "Caroline, Nicole, both of you. When you turn eighteen, you'll both be able to choose your own path, one that works for you. Until then, please try to appreciate this experience, the nature, the tranquility, the glory of these surroundings..." I stopped mid-sentence...*Glory...what a perfect name to describe my mother. River, Uncle Jacob, Aunt Fern, friends who shared this land and her life...they all knew how special she was from the beginning and what has taken me all this time to understand.*

I halted the discussion with my girls that would go nowhere, just as it had gone nowhere with me when I was their age. In that moment, the words I preached to my bored and disinterested audience turned into a silent realization of my own.

EPILOGUE

As we approached the long drive, the chatter from the back seat ceased. In silence, we inched closer to the top of the hill.

I could see my father waiting on the front porch with Uncle Jacob and Aunt Fern. Andrew pulled into one of the open spaces and, without a word, the four of us piled out of the car and took the next few steps in tandem.

Caroline and Nicole managed to perk up as soon as they smelled the aroma drifting past. Unmistakable. Glory's biscuits.

I rushed to greet River and fell easily into his outstretched arms, strong in contrast to the gentle tone of his voice. "Welcome home, my girl," he said. "Welcome home."

Acknowledgements

To my son, Christopher, who humored and encouraged me to learn new tricks and test the unfamiliar waters of writing, publishing and promoting in a world filled with complicated technology. No matter how much I bugged him or how many questions I asked, he was always there for me.

To my daughter, Erin, who reassured me that I shouldn't let the challenges of this industry prevent me from tackling a second novel. It was her enthusiasm with the first rough chapters that persuaded me to finish and publish MY NAME IS ROSE.

To my family of many generations who kept my momentum going with their positive comments and kind words, even as I questioned if I was qualified to compose a story from the heart that would resonate with an audience of young readers.

To the brilliant ladies – my young wizards – of ACORN PUBLISHING, Jessica Therrien, Holly Kammier and Lacey Impellizeri. From start to finish, they wrapped their arms around me and provided me with the tools and knowledge to create a polished manuscript that sparkles and shines. A special thank you to Debra Kennedy, who formatted and understood my vision for bringing each page to life.

To my wonderful editor, Laura Taylor, who made me believe I can write and that my intuitive sense of the human spirit created an inspirational story for all ages.

To DAMONZA – the cover speaks for itself. Thank you for listening to me as we adjusted one revision after another to create the stunning, final version.

To my friends, old and new, near and far, who energized me throughout this process with their sincere and thought-provoking remarks. Their continued validation of my writing abilities convinced me that becoming an author was not a frivolous goal, but a gift I should pursue.

To the entire circle of current and future readers of KEEP FOREVER and MY NAME IS ROSE. You are the reason writers write and why millions of books, in multiple formats, still exist.

And finally, to Jeff, who unwittingly inspired the writer inside of me. I think he would be proud.

Also By Alexa Kingaard

KEEP FOREVER
A fictional story about a Vietnam veteran
and the burden he brings home.

27037785R00144

Made in the USA
San Bernardino, CA
25 February 2019